Pam Houston's first book, *Cowboys are my Weakness* was published to great acclaim in 1993, and has been translated into eight languages. Virago also publish her most recent work of fiction, *Waltzing the Cat* and a collection of essays on adventures in the wild, *A Rough Guide to the Heart*.

She lives in a high valley in Colorado.

D1429822

Cowboys Are My Weakness

Pam Houston

A *Virago* Book

First published by Virago Press 1993

Reprinted 1994, 1999, 2000

Copyright © Pam Houston 1992

The moral right of the author has been asserted

A CIP catalogue record for this book
is available from the British Library

ISBN 1 85381 731 7

Printed and bound in Great Britain by
Clays Ltd, St Ives plc

Virago Press
A Division of
Little, Brown and Company (UK)
Brettenham House
Lancaster Place
London WC2E 7EN

Acknowledgments

The stories in this collection appeared in the following publications:

Cimarron Review, "For Bo"
The Gettysburg Review, "Highwater"
Lodestar, "A Blizzard Under Blue Sky"
Mademoiselle, "Selway" (as "Call of the Wild Man"),
   "In My Next Life" (as "A Woman of Spirit")
Mirabella, "Jackson Is Only One of My Dogs,"
   "Sometimes You Talk About Idaho"
Quarterly West, "How to Talk to a Hunter"

"How to Talk to a Hunter" also appeared in *Best American Short Stories 1990*
   (Richard Ford, guest editor)

This is for Michael

With thanks, also,
to my mother and father,
and to Carol Houck Smith

Contents

Cowboys Are My Weakness

How to Talk to a Hunter

When he says "Skins or blankets?" it will take you a moment to realize that he's asking which you want to sleep under. And in your hesitation he'll decide that he wants to see your skin wrapped in the big black moose hide. He carried it, he'll say, soaking wet and heavier than a dead man, across the tundra for two—was it hours or days or weeks? But the payoff, now, will be to see it fall across one of your white breasts. It's December, and your skin is never really warm, so you will pull the bulk of it around you and pose for him, pose for his camera, without having to narrate this moose's death.

You will spend every night in this man's bed without asking yourself why he listens to top-forty country. Why he donated money to the Republican Party. Why he won't play back his messages while you are in the room. You are there so often the messages pile up. Once you noticed the bright green counter reading as high as fifteen.

He will have lured you here out of a careful independence that you spent months cultivating; though it will finally be winter, the dwindling daylight and the threat of Christmas, that makes you give in. Spending nights with this man means suffering the long face of your sheepdog, who likes to sleep on your bed, who worries when you don't come home. But the hunter's house is so much warmer than yours, and he'll give you a key, and just like a woman, you'll think that means something. It will snow hard for thirteen straight days. Then it will really get cold. When it is sixty below there will be no wind and no clouds, just still air and cold sunshine. The sun on the windows will lure you out of bed, but he'll pull you back under. The next two hours he'll devote to your body. With his hands, with his tongue, he'll express what will seem to you like the most eternal of loves. Like the house key, this is just another kind of lie. Even in bed; especially in bed, you and he cannot speak the same language. The machine will answer the incoming calls. From under an ocean of passion and hide and hair you'll hear a woman's muffled voice between the beeps.

Your best female friend will say, "So what did you think? That a man who sleeps under a dead moose is capable of commitment?"

This is what you learned in college: A man desires the satisfaction of his desire; a woman desires the condition of desiring.

The hunter will talk about spring in Hawaii, summer in Alaska. The man who says he was always better at math will form the sentences so carefully it will be impossible to tell if you are included in these plans. When he asks you if you would like to open a small guest ranch way out in the country, understand that this is a rhetorical question. Label these conversations future perfect, but don't expect the present to catch up with them. Spring is an inconceivable distance from the December days that just keep getting shorter and gray.

He'll ask you if you've ever shot anything, if you'd like to, if you ever thought about teaching your dog to retrieve. Your dog will like him too much, will drop the stick at his feet every time, will roll over and let the hunter scratch his belly.

One day he'll leave you sleeping to go split wood or get the mail and his phone will ring again. You'll sit very still while a woman who calls herself something like Janie Coyote leaves a message on his machine: She's leaving work, she'll say, and the last thing she wanted to hear was the sound of his beautiful voice. Maybe she'll talk only in rhyme. Maybe the counter will change to sixteen. You'll look a question at the mule deer on the wall, and the dark spots on either side of his mouth will tell you he shares more with this hunter than you ever will. One night, drunk, the hunter told you he was sorry for taking that deer, that every now and then there's an animal that isn't meant to be taken, and he should have known that deer was one.

Your best male friend will say, "No one who needs to call herself Janie Coyote can hold a candle to you, but why not let him sleep alone a few nights, just to make sure?"

The hunter will fill your freezer with elk burger, venison sausage, organic potatoes, fresh pecans. He'll tell you to wear your seat belt, to dress warmly, to drive safely. He'll say you are always on his mind, that you're the best thing that's ever happened to him, that you make him glad that he's a man.

Tell him it don't come easy, tell him freedom's just another word for nothing left to lose.

These are the things you'll know without asking: The coyote woman wears her hair in braids. She uses words like "howdy." She's man enough to shoot a deer.

A week before Christmas you'll rent *It's a Wonderful Life* and watch it together, curled on your couch, faces touching. Then you'll bring up the word "monogamy." He'll tell you how badly he was hurt by your predecessor. He'll tell you he couldn't be happier spending every night with you. He'll say there's just a few questions he doesn't have the answers for. He'll say he's just scared and confused. Of course this isn't exactly what he means. Tell him you understand. Tell him you are scared too. Tell him to take all the time he needs. Know that you could never shoot an animal; and be glad of it.

Your best female friend will say, "You didn't tell him you loved him, did you?" Don't even tell her the truth. If you do you'll have to tell her that he said this: "I feel exactly the same way."

Your best male friend will say, "Didn't you know what would happen when you said the word 'commitment'?"

But that isn't the word that you said.

He'll say, "Commitment, monogamy, it all means just one thing."

The coyote woman will come from Montana with the heavier snows. The hunter will call you on the day of the solstice to say he has a friend in town and can't see you. He'll leave you hanging your Christmas lights; he'll give new meaning to the phrase "longest night of the year." The man who has said he's not so good with words will manage to say eight things about his friend without using a gender-determining pronoun. Get out of the house quickly. Call the most understanding person you know who will let you sleep in his bed.

Your best female friend will say, "So what did you think? That he was capable of living outside his gender?"

When you get home in the morning there's a candy tin on your pillow. Santa, obese and grotesque, fondles two small children on the lid. The card will say something like "From your not-so-secret admirer." Open it. Examine each carefully made truffle. Feed them, one at a time, to the dog. Call the hunter's machine. Tell him you don't speak chocolate.

Your best female friend will say, "At this point, what is it about him that you could possibly find appealing?"

Your best male friend will say, "Can't you understand that this is a good sign? Can't you understand that this proves how deep he's in with you?" Hug your best male friend. Give him the truffles the dog wouldn't eat.

Of course the weather will cooperate with the coyote woman. The highways will close, she will stay another night. He'll tell her he's going to work so he can come and see you.

He'll even leave her your number and write "Me at Work" on the yellow pad of paper by his phone. Although you shouldn't, you'll have to be there. It will be you and your nauseous dog and your half-trimmed tree all waiting for him like a series of questions.

This is what you learned in graduate school: In every assumption is contained the possibility of its opposite.

In your kitchen he'll hug you like you might both die there. Sniff him for coyote. Don't hug him back.

He will say whatever he needs to to win. He'll say it's just an old friend. He'll say the visit was all the friend's idea. He'll say the night away from you has given him time to think about how much you mean to him. Realize that nothing short of sleeping alone will ever make him realize how much you mean to him. He'll say that if you can just be a little patient, some good will come out of this for the two of you after all. He still won't use a gender-specific pronoun.

Put your head in your hands. Think about what it means to be patient. Think about the beautiful, smart, strong, clever woman you thought he saw when he looked at you. Pull on your hair. Rock your body back and forth. Don't cry.

He'll say that after holding you it doesn't feel right holding anyone else. For "holding," substitute "fucking." Then take it as a compliment.

He will get frustrated and rise to leave. He may or may not be bluffing. Stall for time. Ask a question he can't immediately answer. Tell him you want to make love on the floor. When he tells you your body is beautiful say, "I feel exactly the same way." Don't, under any circumstances, stand in front of the door.

Your best female friend will say, "They lie to us, they cheat on us, and we love them more for it." She'll say, "It's our fault; we raise them to be like that."

Tell her it can't be your fault. You've never raised anything but dogs.

The hunter will say it's late and he has to go home to sleep. He'll emphasize the last word in the sentence. Give him one kiss that he'll remember while he's fucking the coyote woman. Give him one kiss that ought to make him cry if he's capable of it, but don't notice when he does. Tell him to have a good night.

Your best male friend will say, "We all do it. We can't help it. We're self-destructive. It's the old bad-boy routine. You have a male dog, don't you?"

The next day the sun will be out and the coyote woman will leave. Think about how easy it must be for a coyote woman and a man who listens to top-forty country. The coyote woman would never use a word like "monogamy"; the coyote woman will stay gentle on his mind.

If you can, let him sleep alone for at least one night. If you can't, invite him over to finish trimming your Christmas tree. When he asks how you are, tell him you think it's a good idea to keep your sense of humor during the holidays.

Plan to be breezy and aloof and full of interesting anecdotes about all the other men you've ever known. Plan to be hotter than ever before in bed, and a little cold out of it. Remember that necessity is the mother of invention. Be flexible.

First, he will find the faulty bulb that's been keeping all the others from lighting. He will explain, in great detail, the most elementary electrical principles. You will take turns placing the ornaments you and other men, he and other women, have spent years carefully choosing. Under the circumstances, try to let this be a comforting thought.

He will thin the clusters of tinsel you put on the tree. He'll say something ambiguous like "Next year you should string popcorn and cranberries." Finally, his arm will stretch just high enough to place the angel on the top of the tree.

Your best female friend will say, "Why can't you ever fall in love with a man who will be your friend?"

Your best male friend will say, "You ought to know this by now: Men always cheat on the best women."

This is what you learned in the pop psychology book: Love means letting go of fear.

Play Willie Nelson's "Pretty Paper." He'll ask you to dance, and before you can answer he'll be spinning you around your wood stove, he'll be humming in your ear. Before the song ends he'll be taking off your clothes, setting you lightly under the tree, hovering above you with tinsel in his hair. Through the spread of the branches the all-white lights you insisted on will shudder and blur, outlining the ornaments he brought: a pheasant, a snow goose, a deer.

The record will end. Above the crackle of the wood stove and the rasp of the hunter's breathing you'll hear one long low howl break the quiet of the frozen night: your dog, chained and lonely and cold. You'll wonder if he knows enough to stay in his doghouse. You'll wonder if he knows

Selway

— — — — — — — — — — — — — —

I t was June the seventh and we'd driven eighteen hours of
pavement and sixty miles of dirt to find out the river was at
highwater, the highest of the year, of several years, and rising. The ranger, Ramona, wrote on our permit, "We do not
recommend boating at this level," and then she looked at
Jack.

"We're just gonna go down and take a look at it," he said,
"see if the river gives us a sign." He tried to slide the permit
away from Ramona, but her short dark fingers held it against
the counter. I looked from one to the other. I knew Jack didn't
believe in signs.

"Once you get to Moose Creek you're committed," she
said. "There's no time to change your mind after that. You've
got Double Drop and Little Niagara and Ladle, and they just
keep coming like that, one after another with no slow water in
between."

She was talking about rapids. This was my first northern

trip, and after a lazy spring making slow love between rapids on the wide desert rivers, I couldn't imagine what all the fuss was about.

"If you make it through the Moose Creek series there's only a few more real bad ones; Wolf Creek is the worst. After that the only thing to worry about is the takeout point. The beach will be under water, and if you miss it, you're over Selway Falls."

"Do you have a river guide?" Jack said, and when she bent under the counter to get one he tried again to slide the permit away. She pushed a small, multifolded map in his direction.

"Don't rely on it," she said. "The rapids aren't even marked in the right place."

"Thanks for your help," Jack said. He gave the permit a sharp tug and put it in his pocket.

"There was an accident today," Ramona said. "In Ladle."

"Anybody hurt?" Jack asked.

"It's not official."

"Killed?"

"The water's rising," Ramona said, and turned back to her desk.

At the put-in, the water crashed right over the top of the depth gauge. The grass grew tall and straight through the slats of the boat ramp.

"Looks like we're the first ones this year," Jack said.

The Selway has the shortest season of any river in North America. They don't plow the snow till the first week in June, and by the last week in July there's not enough water to carry a boat. They only allow one party a day on the river that they select from a nationwide lottery with thousands of applicants each year. You can try your whole life and never get a permit.

"Somebody's been here," I said. "The people who flipped today."

Jack didn't answer. He was looking at the gauge. "It's up even from this morning," he said. "They said this morning it was six feet."

Jack and I have known each other almost a year. I'm the fourth in a series of long-term girlfriends he's never gotten around to proposing to. He likes me because I'm young enough not to sweat being single and I don't put pressure on him the way the others did. They wanted him to quit running rivers, to get a job that wasn't seasonal, to raise a family like any man his age. They wouldn't go on trips with him, not even once to see what it was like, and I couldn't imagine that they knew him in any way that was complete if they hadn't known him on the river, if they hadn't seen him row.

I watched him put his hand in the water. "Feel that, baby," he said. "That water was snow about fifteen minutes ago."

I stuck my foot in the water and it went numb in about ten seconds. I've been to four years of college and I should know better, but I love it when he calls me baby.

Jack has taken a different highwater trip each year for the last fifteen, on progressively more difficult rivers. When a river is at high water it's not just deeper and faster and colder than usual. It's got a different look and feel from the rest of the year. It's dark and impatient and turbulent, like a volcano or a teenage boy. It strains against its banks and it churns around and under itself. Looking at its fullness made me want to grab Jack and throw him down on the boat ramp and make love right next to where the river roared by, but I could tell by his face he was trying to make a decision, so I sat and stared at the river and wondered if it was this wild at the put-in what it would look like in the rapids.

"If anything happened to you . . ." he said, and threw a stick out to the middle of the channel. "It must be moving nine miles an hour." He walked up and down the boat ramp. "What do you think?" he said.

"I think this is a chance of a lifetime," I said. "I think you're the best boatman you know." I wanted to feel the turbulence underneath me. I wanted to run a rapid that could flip a boat. I hadn't taken anything like a risk in months. I wanted to think about dying.

It was already early evening, and once we made the decision to launch, there were two hours of rigging before we could get on the water. On the southern rivers we'd boat sometimes for an hour after dark just to watch what the moon did to the water. On the Selway there was a rapid that could flip your boat around every corner. It wasn't getting pitch dark till ten-thirty that far north, where the June dusk went on forever, but it wasn't really light either and we wouldn't be able to see very far ahead. We told ourselves we'd go a tenth of a mile and make camp, but you can't camp on a sheer granite wall, and the river has to give you a place to get stopped and get tied.

I worked fast and silent, wondering if we were doing the right thing and knowing if we died it would really be my fault, because as much as I knew Jack wanted to go, he wouldn't have pushed me if I'd said I was scared. Jack was untamable, but he had some sense and a lot of respect for the river. He relied on me to speak with the voice of reason, to be life-protecting because I'm a woman and that's how he thinks women are, but I've never been protective enough of anything, least of all myself.

At nine-fifteen we untied the rope and let the river take us. "The first place that looks campable," Jack said.

Nine miles an hour is fast in a rubber raft on a river you've never boated when there's not quite enough light to see what's in front of you. We were taking on water over the bow almost immediately, even though the map didn't show any rapids for the first two miles. It was hard for me to take my eyes off Jack, the way his muscles strained with every stroke, first his upper arms, then his upper thighs. He was silent, thinking it'd been a mistake to come, but I was laughing and bailing water and combing the banks for a flat spot and jumping back and forth over my seat to kiss him, and watching while his muscles flexed.

My mother says I thrive on chaos, and I guess that's true, because as hard a year as I've had with Jack I stayed with it, and I won't even admit by how much the bad days outnumbered the good. We fought like bears when we weren't on the river, because he was so used to fighting and I was so used to getting my own way. I said I wanted selfless devotion and he took a stand on everything from infidelity to salad dressing, and it was always opposite to mine. The one thing we had going for us, though, was the sex, and if we could stop screaming at each other long enough to make love it would be a day or sometimes two before something would happen and we'd go at it again. I've always been afraid to stop and think too hard about what great sex in bad times might mean, but it must have something to do with timing, that moment making love when you're at once absolutely powerful and absolutely helpless, a balance we could never find when we were out of bed.

It was the old southern woman next door, the hunter's

widow, who convinced me I should stay with him each time I'd get mad enough to leave. She said if I didn't have to fight for him I'd never know if he was mine. She said the wild ones were the only ones worth having and that I had to let him do whatever it took to keep him wild. She said I wouldn't love him if he ever gave in, and the harder I looked at my life, the more I saw a series of men—wild in their own way—who thought because I said I wanted security and commitment, I did. Sometimes it seems this simple: I tamed them and made them dull as fence posts and left each one for someone wilder than the last. Jack is the wildest so far, and the hardest, and even though I've been proposed to sixteen times, five times by men I've never made love to, I want him all to myself and at home more than I've ever wanted anything.

"Are you bailing? I'm standing in water back here," he said, so I bailed faster but the waves kept on crashing over the bow.

"I can't move this boat," he said, which I knew wasn't entirely true, but it was holding several hundred gallons of water times eight pounds a gallon, and that's more weight than I'd care to push around.

"There," he said. "Camp. Let's try to get to shore."

He pointed to a narrow beach a hundred yards down-stream. The sand looked black in the twilight; it was long and flat enough for a tent.

"Get the rope ready," he said. "You're gonna have to jump for it and find something to wrap around fast."

He yelled *jump* but it was too early and I landed chest-deep in the water and the cold took my breath but I scrambled across the rocks to the beach and wrapped around a fallen trunk just as the rope went tight. The boat dragged the trunk and me ten yards down the beach before Jack could get out and pull the nose of it up on shore.

"This may have been real fuckin' stupid," he said.

I wanted to tell him how the water made me feel, how horny and crazy and happy I felt riding on top of water that couldn't hold itself in, but he was scared, for the first time since I'd known him, so I kept my mouth shut and went to set up the tent.

In the morning the tent was covered all around with a thin layer of ice and we made love like crazy people, the way you do when you think it might be the last time ever, till the sun changed the ice back to dew and got the tent so hot we were sweating. Then Jack got up and made coffee, and we heard the boaters coming just in time to get our clothes on.

They threw us their rope and we caught it. There were three of them, three big men in a boat considerably bigger than ours. Jack poured them coffee. We all sat down on the fallen log.

"You launched late last night?" the tallest, darkest one said. He had curly black hair and a wide open face.

Jack nodded. "Too late," he said. "Twilight boating."

"It's up another half a foot this morning," the man said. "It's supposed to peak today at seven."

The official forest service document declares the Selway unsafe for boating above six feet. Seven feet is off their charts.

"Have you boated this creek at seven?" Jack asked. The man frowned and took a long drink from his cup.

"My name's Harvey," he said, and stuck out his hand. "This is Charlie and Charlie. We're on a training trip." He laughed. "Yahoo."

Charlie and Charlie nodded.

"You know the river," Jack said.

"I've boated the Selway seventy times," he said. "Never at seven feet. It was all the late snow and last week's heat wave. It's a bad combination, but it's boatable. This river's always boatable if you know exactly where to be."

Charlie and Charlie smiled.

"There'll be a lot of holes that there's no way to miss. You got to punch through them."

Jack nodded. I knew Harvey was talking about boat flippers. Big waves that form in holes the river makes behind rocks and ledges and that will suck boats in and hold them there, fill them with water till they flip, hold bodies, too, indefinitely, until they go under and catch the current, or until the hole decides to spit them out. If you hit a hole with a back wave bigger than your boat perfectly straight, there's a half a chance you'll shoot through. A few degrees off in either direction, and the hole will get you every time.

"We'll be all right in this tank," Harvey said, nodding to his boat, "but I'm not sure I'd run it in a boat that small. I'm not sure I'd run it in a boat I had to bail."

Unlike ours, Harvey's boat was a self-bailer, inflatable tubes around an open metal frame that let the water run right through. They're built for high water, and extremely hard to flip.

"Just the two of you?" Harvey said.

Jack nodded.

"A honeymoon trip. Nice."

"We're not married," Jack said.

"Yeah," Harvey said. He picked up a handful of sand. "The black sand of the Selway," he said. "I carried a bottle of this sand downriver the year I got married. I wanted to throw

it at my wife's feet during the ceremony. The minister thought
it was pretty strange, but he got over it."

One of the Charlies looked confused.

"Black sand," Harvey said. "You know, black sand, love,
marriage, Selway, rivers, life; the whole thing."

I smiled at Jack, but he wouldn't meet my eyes.

"You'll be all right till Moose Creek," Harvey said.
"That's when it gets wild. We're gonna camp there tonight,
run the bad stretch first thing in the morning in case we wrap
or flip or tear something. I hope you won't think I'm insulting
you if I ask you to run with us. It'll be safer for us both. The
people who flipped yesterday were all experienced. They all
knew the Selway."

"They lost one?" Jack said.

"Nobody will say for sure," Harvey said. "But I'd bet on
it."

"We'll think about it," Jack said. "It's nice of you to offer."

"I know what you're thinking," Harvey said. "But I've got
a kid now. It makes a difference." He pulled a picture out of
his wallet. A baby girl, eight or nine months old, crawled
across a linoleum floor.

"She's beautiful," I said.

"She knocks me out," Harvey said. "She follows everything with her finger; bugs, flowers, the TV, you know what I
mean?"

Jack and I nodded.

"It's your decision," he said. "Maybe we'll see you at
Moose Creek."

He stood up, and Charlie and Charlie rose behind him. One
coiled the rope while the other pushed off.

Jack poured his third cup of coffee. "Think he's full of
shit?" he said.

"I think he knows more than you or I ever will," I said.

"About this river, at least," he said.

"At least," I said.

In midday sunshine, the river looked more fun than terrify-ing. We launched just before noon, and though there was no time for sightseeing I bailed fast enough to let Jack move the boat through the rapids, which came quicker and bigger around every bend. The map showed ten rapids between the put-in and Moose Creek, and it was anybody's guess which of the fifty or sixty rapids we boated that day were the ones the forest service had in mind. Some had bigger waves than oth-ers, some narrower passages, but the river was continuous moving white water, and we finally put the map away. On the southern rivers we'd mix rum and fruit juice and eat smoked oysters and pepper cheese. Here, twenty fast miles went by without time to take a picture, to get a drink of water. The Moose Creek pack bridge came into sight, and we pulled in and tied up next to Harvey's boat.

"White fuckin' water," Harvey said. "Did you have a good run?"

"No trouble," Jack said.

"Good," Harvey said. "Here's where she starts to kick ass." He motioned with his head downriver. "We'll get up at dawn and scout everything."

"It's early yet," Jack said. "I think we're going on." I looked at Jack's face, and then Harvey's.

"You do what you want," Harvey said. "But you ought to take a look at the next five miles. The runs are obvious once you see them from the bank, but they change at every level."

"We haven't scouted all day," Jack said. I knew he wanted us to run alone, that he thought following Harvey would be cheating somehow, but I believed a man who'd throw sand at his new wife's feet, and I liked a little danger but I didn't want to die.

"There's only one way through Ladle," Harvey said. "Ladle's where they lost the girl."

"The girl?" Jack said.

"The rest of her party was here when we got here. Their boats were below Ladle. They just took off, all but her husband. He wouldn't leave, and you can't blame him. He was rowing when she got tossed. He let the boat get sideways. He's been wandering around here for two days, I guess, but he wouldn't get back in the boat."

"Jesus Christ," Jack said. He sat down on the bank facing the water.

I looked back into the woods for the woman's husband and tried to imagine a posture for him, tried to imagine an expression for his face. I thought about my Uncle Tim, who spent ten years and a lifetime of savings building his dream home. On the day it was completed he backed his pickup over his four-year-old daughter while she played in the driveway. He sold the house in three days and went completely gray in a week.

"A helicopter landed about an hour ago," Harvey said. "Downstream, where the body must be. It hasn't taken off."

"The water's still rising," Jack said, and we all looked to where we'd pulled the boats up on shore and saw that they were floating. And then we heard the beating of the propeller and saw the helicopter rising out over the river. We saw the hundred feet of cable hanging underneath it and then we saw the woman, arched like a dancer over the thick black belt they must use for transplanting wild animals, her long hair dangling, her arms slung back. The pilot flew up the river till he'd gained enough altitude, turned back, and headed over the mountain wall behind our camp.

"They said she smashed her pelvis against a rock and bled to death internally," Harvey said. "They got her out in less than three minutes, and it was too late."

Jack put his arm around my knees. "We'll scout at dawn," he said. "We'll all run this together."

Harvey was up rattling coffeepots before we had time to make love and I said it would bring us bad luck if we didn't but Jack said it would be worse than bad luck if we didn't scout the rapids. The scouting trail was well worn. Harvey went first, then Jack, then me and the two Charlies. Double Drop was first, two sets of falls made by water pouring over clusters of house-sized boulders that extended all the way across the river.

"You can sneak the first drop on the extreme right," Harvey said. "There's no sneak for the second. Just keep her straight and punch her through. Don't let her get you sideways."

Little Niagara was a big drop, six feet or more, but the run was pretty smooth and the back wave low enough to break through.

"Piece of cake," Harvey said.

The sun was almost over the canyon wall, and we could hear Ladle long before we rounded the bend. I wasn't prepared for what I saw. One hundred yards of white water stretched from shore to shore and thundered over rocks and logjams and ledges. There were ten holes the size of the one in Double Drop, and there was no space for a boat in between. The currents were so chaotic for such a long stretch there was no way to read which way they'd push a boat. We found some small logs and climbed a rock ledge that hung over the rapid.

"See if you can read this current," Harvey said, and tossed the smallest log into the top of the rapid. The log hit the first hole and went under. It didn't come back up. One of the Charlies giggled.

"Again," Harvey said. This time the log came out of the first hole and survived two more before getting swallowed by the biggest hole, about midway through the rapid.

"I'd avoid that one for sure," Harvey said. "Try to get left of that hole." He threw the rest of the logs in. None of them made it through. "This is big-time," he said.

We all sat on the rock for what must have been an hour. "Seen enough?" Harvey said. "We've still got No Slouch and Miranda Jane."

The men climbed down off the rock, but I wasn't quite ready to leave. I went to the edge of the ledge, lay flat on my stomach, and hung over until my head was so full of the roar of the river I got dizzy and pulled myself back up. The old southern woman said men can't really live unless they face death now and then, and I know by men she didn't mean mankind. And I wondered which rock shattered the dead woman's pelvis, and I wondered what she and I were doing out here on this river when Harvey's wife was home with that beautiful baby and happy. And I knew it was crazy to take a boat through that rapid and I knew I'd do it anyway but I didn't any longer know why. Jack said I had to do it for myself to make it worth anything, and at first I thought I was there because I loved danger, but sitting on the rock I knew I was there because I loved Jack. And maybe I went because his old girlfriends wouldn't, and maybe I went because I wanted him for mine, and maybe it didn't matter at all why I went because doing it for me and doing it for him amounted, finally, to exactly the same thing. And even though I knew in my head there's nothing a man can do that a woman can't, I also knew in my heart we can't help doing it for different reasons. And just like a man will never understand exactly how a woman feels when she has a baby, or an orgasm, or the reasons why she'll fight so hard to be loved, a woman can't know in what way a man satisfies himself, what question he answers for himself, when he looks right at death.

My head was so full of the sound and the light of the river that when I climbed down off the bank side of the ledge I didn't see the elk carcass until I stepped on one of its curled hooves. It was a young elk, probably not dead a year, and still mostly covered with matted brown fur. The skull was picked clean by scavengers, polished white by the sun and grinning. The sound that came out of my mouth scared me as much as the elk had, and I felt silly a few minutes later when Harvey came barreling around the corner followed by Jack.

Harvey saw the elk and smiled.

"It startled me is all," I said.

"Jesus," Jack said. "Stay with us, all right?"

"I never scream," I said. "Hardly ever."

No Slouch and Miranda Jane were impressive rapids, but they were nothing like Ladle and both runnable to the left. On the way back to camp we found wild strawberries, and Jack and I hung back and fed them to each other and I knew he wasn't mad about me screaming. The boats were loaded by ten-thirty and the sun was warm. We wore life jackets and helmets and wet suits. Everybody had diver's boots but me, so I wore my loafers.

"You have three minutes in water this cold," Harvey said. "Even with a wet suit. Three minutes before hypothermia starts, and then you can't swim, and then you just give in to the river."

Harvey gave us the thumbs-up sign as the Charlies pushed off. I pushed off right behind them. Except for the bail bucket and the spare oar, everything on the boat was tied down twice and inaccessible. My job was to take water out of the boat as fast as I could eight pounds at a time, and to help Jack remember which rapid was coming next and where we had decided to run it.

I saw the first of the holes in Double Drop and yelled, "Right," and we made the sneak with a dry boat. We got turned around somehow after that, though, and had to hit the big wave backwards. Jack yelled, "Hang on, baby," and we hit it straight on and it filled the boat, but then we were through it and in sight of Little Niagara before I could even start bailing.

"We're going twelve miles an hour at least," Jack yelled. "Which one is this?"

"Niagara," I yelled. "Right center." The noise of the river swallowed my words and I only threw out two bucketfuls before we were over the lip of Niagara and I had to hold on. I could hear Ladle around the bend and I was throwing water so fast I lost my balance and that's when I heard Jack say, "Bail faster!" and that's when I threw the bail bucket into the river and watched, unbelieving, as it went under, and I saw Jack see it too but we were at Ladle and I had to sit down and hold on. I watched Harvey's big boat getting bounced around like a cork, and I think I closed my eyes when the first wave crashed over my face because the next thing I knew we were out of the heaviest water and Harvey was standing and smiling at us with his fist in the air.

I could see No Slouch around the bend and I don't remember it or Miranda Jane because I was kneeling in the front of the boat scooping armfuls of water the whole time.

We all pulled up on the first beach we found and drank a beer and hugged each other uncertainly, like tenants in an apartment building where the fires have been put out.

"You're on your own," Harvey said. "We're camping here. Take a look at Wolf Creek, and be sure and get to shore before Selway Falls." He picked up a handful of black sand and let it run through his fingers. He turned to me. "He's a good boatman, and you're very brave."

I smiled.

"Take care of each other," he said. "Stay topside."

We set off alone and it clouded up and started to rain and I couldn't make the topography match the river map.

"I can't tell where we are," I told Jack. "But Wolf Creek can't be far."

"We'll see it coming," he said, "or hear it."

But it wasn't five minutes after he spoke that we rounded a bend and were in it, waves crashing on all sides and Jack trying to find a way between the rocks and the holes. I was looking too, and I think I saw the run, fifty feet to our right, right before I heard Jack say, "Hang on, baby," and we hit the hole sideways and everything went white and cold. I was in the waves and underwater and I couldn't see Jack or the boat, I couldn't move my arms or legs apart from how the river tossed them. Jack had said swim down to the current, but I couldn't tell which way was down and I couldn't have moved there in that washing machine, my lungs full and taking on water. Then the wave spit me up, once, under the boat, and then again, clear of it, and I got a breath and pulled down away from the air and felt the current grab me, and I waited to get smashed against a rock, but the rock didn't come and I was at the surface riding the crests of some eight-foot rollers and seeing Jack's helmet bobbing in the water in front of me.

"Swim, baby!" he yelled, and it was like it hadn't occurred to me, like I was frozen there in the water. And I tried to swim but I couldn't get a breath and my limbs wouldn't move and I thought about the three minutes and hypothermia and I must have been swimming then because the shore started to get closer. I grabbed the corner of a big ledge and wouldn't let go, not even when Jack yelled at me to get out of the water, and even when he showed me an easy place to get out if I just floated a few yards downstream it took all I had and more to let go of the rock and get back in the river.

I got out on a tiny triangular rock ledge, surrounded on all sides by walls of granite. Jack stood sixty feet above me on another ledge.

"Sit tight," he said. "I'm going to go see if I can get the boat."

Then he was gone and I sat in that small space and started to shake. It was raining harder, sleeting even, and I started to think about freezing to death in that space that wasn't even big enough for me to move around in and get warm. I started to think about the river rising and filling that space and what would happen when Jack got back and made me float downstream to an easier place, or what would happen if he didn't come back, if he died trying to get the boat back, if he chased it fifteen miles to Selway Falls. When I saw the boat float by, right side up and empty, I decided to climb out of the space.

I'd lost one loafer in the river, so I wedged myself between the granite walls and used my fingers, mostly, to climb. I've always been a little afraid of heights, so I didn't look down. I thought it would be stupid to live through the boating accident and smash my skull free-climbing on granite, but as I

inched up the wall I got warmer and kept going. When I got to
the top there were trees growing across, and another vertical
bank I hadn't seen from below. I bashed through the
branches with my helmet and grabbed them one at a time till
they broke or pulled out and then I grabbed the next one
higher. I dug into the thin layer of soil that covered the rock
with my knees and my elbows, and I'd slip down an inch for
every two I gained. When I came close to panic I thought of
Rambo, as if he were a real person, as if what I was doing was
possible, and proven before, by him.

And then I was on the ledge and I could see the river, and I
could see Jack on the other side, and I must have been in
shock, a little, because I couldn't at that time imagine how he
could have gotten to the other side of the river, I couldn't
imagine what would make him go back in the water, but he
had, and there he was on the other side.

"I lost the boat," he yelled. "Walk downstream till you see
it."

I was happy for instructions and I set off down the scouting
trail, shoe on one foot, happy for the pain in the other, happy
to be walking, happy because the sun was trying to come out
again and I was there to see it. It was a few miles before I even
realized that the boat would be going over the falls, that Jack
would have had to swim one more time across the river to get
to the trail, that I should go back and see if he'd made it, but I
kept walking downstream and looking for the boat. After five
miles my bare foot started to bleed, so I put my left loafer on
my right foot and walked on. After eight miles I saw Jack
running up the trail behind me, and he caught up and kissed
me and ran on by.

I walked and I walked, and I thought about being twenty-
one and hiking in mountains not too far from these with a boy

who almost drowned and then proposed to me. His boots had filled with the water of a river even farther to the north, and I was wearing sneakers and have a good kick, so I made it across just fine. I thought about how he sat on the far bank after he'd pulled himself out and shivered and stared at the water. And how I ran up and down the shore looking for the shallowest crossing, and then, thinking I'd found it, met him halfway. I remembered when our hands touched across the water and how I'd pulled him to safety and built him a fire and dried his clothes. Later that night he asked me to marry him and it made me happy and I said yes even though I knew it would never happen because I was too young and free and full of my freedom. I switched my loafer to the other foot and wondered if this danger would make Jack propose to me. Maybe he was the kind of man who needed to see death first, maybe we would build a fire to dry ourselves and then he would ask me and I would say yes because by the time you get to be thirty, freedom has circled back on itself to mean something totally different from what it did at twenty-one.

I knew I had to be close to the falls and I felt bad about what the wrecked boat would look like, but all of a sudden it was there in front of me, stuck on a gravel bar in the middle of the river with a rapid on either side, and I saw Jack coming back up the trail toward me.

"I've got it all figured out," he said. "I need to walk upstream about a mile and jump in there. That'll give me enough time to swim most of the way across to the other side of the river, and if I've read the current right, it'll take me right into that gravel bar."

"And if you read the current wrong?" I said.

He grinned. "Then it's over Selway Falls. I almost lost it already the second time I crossed the river. It was just like

Harvey said. I almost gave up. I've been running twelve miles and I know my legs'll cramp. It's a long shot but I've got to take it."

"Are you sure you want to do this?" I said. "Maybe you shouldn't do this."

"I thought the boat was gone," he said, "and I didn't care because you were safe and I was safe and we were on the same side of the river. But there it is asking me to come for it, and the water's gonna rise tonight and take it over the falls. You stay right here where you can see what happens to me. If I make it I'll pick you up on that beach just below. We've got a half a mile to the takeout and the falls." He kissed me again and ran back upriver.

The raft was in full sunshine, everything tied down, oars in place. Even the map I couldn't read was there, where I stuck it, under a strap.

I could see Jack making his way through the trees toward the edge of the river, and I realized then that more than any other reason for being on that trip, I was there because I thought I could take care of him, and maybe there's something women want to protect after all. And maybe Jack's old girlfriends were trying to protect him by making him stay home, and maybe I thought I could if I was there, but as he dropped out of sight and into the water I knew there'd always be places he'd go that I couldn't, and that I'd have to let him go, just like the widow said. Then I saw his tiny head in the water and I held my breath and watched his position, which was perfect, as he approached the raft. But he got off center right at the end, and a wave knocked him past the raft and farther down the gravel bar. He got to his feet and went down again. He grabbed for a boulder on the bottom and got washed even farther away. He was using all his energy to stay in one place and he was fifty yards downriver from the raft. I started to pray then, to whomever I pray to when I get in real trouble, and it may have been a coincidence but he started moving forward. It took him fifteen minutes and strength I'll never know to get to the boat, but he was in it, and rowing, and heading for the beach.

Later, when we were safe and on the two-lane heading home, Jack told me we were never in any real danger, and I let him get away with it because I knew that's what he had to tell himself to get past almost losing me.

"The river gave us both a lesson in respect," he said, and it occurred to me then that he thought he had a chance to tame that wild river, but I knew I was at its mercy from the very beginning, and I thought all along that that was the point.

Jack started telling stories to keep himself awake: the day his kayak held him under for almost four minutes, the time he crashed his hang glider twice in one day. He said he thought fifteen years of highwater was probably enough, and that he'd take desert rivers from now on.

The road stretched out in front of us, dry and even and smooth. We found a long dirt road, turned, and pulled down to where it ended at a chimney that stood tall amid the rubble of an old stone house. We didn't build a fire and Jack didn't propose; we rolled out our sleeping bags and lay down next to the truck. I could see the light behind the mountains in the place where the moon would soon rise, and I thought about all the years I'd spent saying love and freedom were mutually exclusive and living my life as though they were exactly the same thing.

The wind carried the smell of the mountains, high and sweet. It was so still I could imagine a peace without boredom.

Highwater

C asey told me she was pregnant in the same offhand way
that so much of life's most important information is re-
vealed. We were eating black bean and cheese burritos at the
Fat Chihuahua on the west side of town near the lake. I
started to pour her a second beer from the pitcher in front of
me, and she shook her head.

"Only one for me," she said, and then she patted her stomach as if I was supposed to know what she meant, as if it was
some kind of inside joke between us.

"What?" I said, and then she bobbed her head from one
side to the other the way she does when she doesn't want to
answer, and I knew that had been her way of telling me.

"No way," I said.

She nodded, and then she grinned, and then she ordered a
glass of milk so I'd know for sure.

We drove out to the lake just for somewhere to go, to the

place where the beaches used to be before the water started coming up. Now there was only a two-foot strip of land between the lake and the interstate, and it was piled high with sandbags. No one knew why the water was rising, or when it would stop. When the wind blew up across the salt flats, waves as tall as four feet crashed on the highway.

"How long have you known?" I said.

"Two weeks. We conceived on my thirtieth birthday. Can you beat that?" she said. "Biology in action."

It was just like Casey not to tell me right away, to sit on it herself for a while, to get the feel of it before she tried it out on me. I've always said she's the definition of a hedonist, and as much as she can be under those circumstances, she's my best friend. Not that a hedonist is the worst thing you can be. Her boyfriend, Chuck, told her it meant she gave good blow jobs, and she got mad, but after I showed her the real definition she knew it was true and I've even heard her describe herself that way, once or twice since then, to people she didn't know.

I wanted to be honest so I told her I wasn't sure hedonists were supposed to have babies, and she said she thought that it was just about the best a baby could do.

The mountain remnant they call Antelope Island rose out of the lake in front of us like a mirage, and doubled itself perfectly in the still water. Beyond it were the billion-dollar pieces of machinery that would start pumping excess water out of the lake and into the salt flats within the year.

"Does Chuck know?" I asked.

She shook her head.

"What do you think he'll say?"

Chuck lives with Casey in the house behind mine. He isn't just a hedonist, he's a musician. He plays the piano and sings in a real throaty voice in a bar downtown. Casey fell in love with his fingers first. The morning after the first night she went to bed with him she drew me a picture of his hands.

"Millie," she said, "you can't imagine what it's like with someone whose fingers are so long and muscular."

I tried to imagine it, then I stopped.

"Does Richard have long fingers?"

Richard is the man I date. He is compact: a perfect miniature of a perfect man with ice-blue eyes so deep they're hard to measure. His fingers are short, but I'm not that tall. Our sex is fine.

Casey has known Chuck exactly as long as I've known Richard. We met both men on the same weekend, and got together late the next morning for the Sunday report. Besides drawing me a picture of Chuck's fingers, Casey told me these things: Chuck used to be a junkie but now he's clean, he had a one-bedroom basement apartment and one hundred and twenty-seven compact disks, and he used moleskin condoms which don't work as well but feel much better. This is what I told her about Richard: He put marinated asparagus into the salad, he used the expression "laissez-faire capitalist" three times, once in a description of himself, he played a tape called "The Best of One Hundred and One Strings," and as far as I could tell, he'd never had oral sex.

"You're kidding, right?" Casey said.

Once they met, it took Chuck and Casey three weeks to move in together. Chuck showed up on a Saturday morning with his compact disks, three sets of wind chimes, seven musical instruments, and a box full of calendars called "Women on the Move." All twelve months were topped with half-naked pictures of Salt Lake City paramedics, and Chuck's ex-wife was on the cover. If Casey was intimidated by it, it didn't show.

Six months went by before Casey got pregnant, and during that time I only brought up living together once to Richard, and he said then that it was economically and emotionally unfeasible. What he really meant was that he didn't want to end up supporting me and that he was still hung up on his ex-girlfriend, Karen. Every Wednesday night he drove halfway across the state to see her. He said that if I let it bother me, I was too young to understand a real friendship between a woman and a man, but he always took a fifth of Scotch with him that came back empty, and he always wore a necklace that he never wore for me.

Every Thursday morning Richard would show up back at my house looking like a whipped dog, and when I finally got the nerve to ask him about it he said that actually Karen spent most of the time they were together yelling at him for wasting her last four childbearing years. I asked him what that had to do with friendship, and what he expected to gain for himself, and he said he needed to understand the depth of her anger, he needed to get some answers before he could really go on. I told him that for those kinds of questions one answer was as good as another, but he shook his head, and I decided he might think he wanted answers, but really what he wanted was to be forgiven, or maybe something worse.

Karen called his house every day at least once to yell at him some more, and he'd sit on his bed in the dark and never say a word into the phone. I asked him if she yelled about things he'd done while they were together, or just about the way he was, and he shrugged and said, "Both." She didn't like the way he drove, the way he made love, the way he signed his name. If he didn't answer the phone, she'd let it ring a hundred times.

I called her house once to see if she'd have anything to say to me and her answering machine said: "This is Karen, and *obviously* I'm not home." I hung up fast and never had the courage to try again.

Casey and I are exactly the same age and we are both ten years younger than Richard and Chuck. You'd think because they're from the same generation they'd have something in common, but it's like they got on two different buses at birth and just happened to wind up in the same place. Richard was brought up in a wealthy Texas ranching family that was extremely conservative. He spent ten years in Santa Fe, where he learned to get along with liberals, to play the stock market, and to use marinated asparagus to impress a date. Chuck grew up on the beach in Hawaii. He's kind and unreliable and stoned all the time. The only thing the two men have in common is how much smarter and more world-wise they feel than Casey and me. When we were all together we made jokes about father figures and Freud and Oedipal fantasies, but it wasn't really all that funny because Casey's father had died of a heroin overdose, and mine never said he loved me in twenty-nine years.

Chuck took the news about the baby pretty well. He started coming home earlier from the club, and he and Casey would sit outside in the morning and play Yahtzee, and for about two months I was jealous of their happiness. Then Chuck landed a spot with a band that had a gig in Las Vegas and he was gone five days a week, and even though he insisted that it wouldn't last long and that it wasn't related to the baby, I thought it was pretty bad timing and probably not just a coincidence.

I put off telling Richard about Casey's baby, because I knew if I did he'd think I wanted one too, and even though I'd tell him that couldn't be further from the truth he'd believe it anyway. Finally, the three of us had dinner and Casey told him herself and he smiled and acted happy, but then he shot me a look that said it would never work out in a million years. Richard pretended to think that Casey was ill-bred and irresponsible, but I know part of him wished he could be poor and pregnant and unconcerned like she was, and that was the part I loved the most about him, if you boiled it right down.

Chuck was in Las Vegas every Wednesday through Monday, and I know Casey thought pretty hard about what she called the "a" word while he was gone, and even though I wanted to give Chuck the benefit of the doubt, I thought it might be the best thing she could do.

"Even Richard believes in abortion," I told her.

"All that means is that he got somebody pregnant that he didn't want to marry," she said.

"That must have been Stephanie," I said. "The one before Karen. We went to her house once. She still has pictures of him all over her walls. It's been almost seven years."

"Be careful, Millie," she said.

There was a Lamaze class on Thursday nights and I offered to fill in for Chuck until the Las Vegas deal was over, but Casey wasn't interested in going.

"I'm reading all about it," she said, as if she were an avid reader, as if I'd ever known her to finish a book.

"Have you heard from Chuck?" I asked. It was Tuesday morning. He should have been home. I watched her head bob back and forth.

"You know what I can't figure out?" she said.

"Hmm."

"I can't figure out those women who find out they're pregnant and they just slip into motherhood like they've been waiting for it their whole lives. Their voice starts changing, and they start knitting like they were born doing it. How does that happen? Why didn't it happen to me?"

"Maybe it takes a few months," I said. "Maybe the idea will grow on you."

"Millie," she said, "in five months a doctor is going to hand me a baby and I'm going to have to bring it home. I guess when it's right here in front of me I'll know what to do, but sometimes I look down at my stomach and I feel it move and I think my God it's some kind of alien or something."

"Do you think it's going to hurt a lot?" I said.

She shrugged. "What's a little pain. It's not like it goes on forever."

"They say it's like really bad cramps," I said.

"Then how bad could it be?"

Pretty bad, I thought, but next to Casey I'm a weakling, and who knew how bad the pain would have to be to get to her. She didn't have any insurance, and at first she wanted to have the baby at home, but the doctor wanted her in the hospital and she finally said that money and babies weren't worth killing yourself over, and gave in.

"One thing about it," I said, "is when it's all over you'll have something that's really yours, something that has to love you more than anyone else. You'll have something that won't

ever leave you, or at least not really leave you, at least not for
eighteen years."

"But what if I don't love it?" she said.

Casey and I were celebrating the first night of her sixth
month when Richard came by without calling. He said he
wanted to go for a drive and talk about our future, and even
though his visits to Karen had increased to two nights a week,
and even though she was calling now two or three times a day,
I took it as a good sign.

He didn't talk the whole way out to the lake, but when we
got close to the place where you turn off the highway he held
my hand and I could feel his muscles, tight all the way to the
back of his neck.

The lake was calm and it reflected headlights from the
interstate halfway to Nevada. If I squinted I could make out
the silhouette of the turrets that crowned the palace they used
to call the Saltair. Inside the dark building the water was
higher than the second floor.

"So." His voice made me jump. "What do you think our
potential is in the long-long run?" It sounded like stocks.

"In the long-long run," I said, "I think our potential is
good." His free hand drummed the dashboard.

"Do you think I can satisfy you, sexually and otherwise, for
a long time?"

I said, "I think you can satisfy me for a long time." The
veins around his temples looked like they would burst.

"Does it bother you," he said, "that I'm a little older than
you?"

"Not in the least," I said.

He drew in a breath. "Do you want to have children?"

I didn't know the answer.

"I think so," I said, "someday. Do you?"

"I never thought so," he said. "But now I do. The only question is . . ."

"With who?" I said.

"I know that sounds awful," he said, "but I had to know how you felt."

Never cry in front of him, Casey said, but I did, entirely too often.

"Now that I know how you feel I can get things settled with Karen, and then you and I will go on a trip."

For a minute the idea of a trip cheered me up, but then I started to think about how we never had a conversation about our future that didn't have Karen's name in it. I started to think about how disgusted Casey would be with me if she heard what he'd said, and I even started to think about getting out of the car. But all that was out there was salt water and highway, so I waited for him to stop thinking long enough to drive me home.

It was the beginning of Casey's seventh month and everything about her was changing, her jawline especially, and her eyes.

"So how's Richard?" she said. "I haven't seen him lately."

"I haven't either," I said, and it was true. He'd been seeing more of Karen than ever, and even though I tried to be grown-up about it I always wound up crying and acting like the child he thought I was. He said sometimes I was even harder to deal with than she was, and that he needed some time alone to figure things out, but time alone always turned out to mean time with Karen, and things wouldn't ever get figured out until he decided to leave them alone.

Casey told me to tell him to get it straight with Karen and

call me when he was finished, and I did. But he said he couldn't stand to be without me for that long and I said how long and he said it wouldn't be much longer at all. He was spending three nights a week with each of us; the seventh night swung back and forth.

"How long are you gonna do this?" Casey said.

"This week is Karen's fortieth birthday," I said. "He thinks she might go over the edge."

"What about you?"

"He says I need to be strong and patient and mature. He says if I can be all of those things he'll get it worked out much faster."

"Dump him, Millie." Casey rolled her hands over and over her belly. Chuck had been gone for three weeks straight. I didn't ask her if he'd called, but if he had she would have told me.

"He says we're going to go to Santa Fe together," I said. "I've always wanted to go to Santa Fe. As soon as it's all worked out, that's where we're going to go."

"Oh, Millie."

"He's not sleeping with her," I said.

"How do you know?"

"I count his condoms."

She smiled.

"Before he leaves, and then again when he comes back."

"I bet that makes you feel pretty good about yourself," she said, and then when she saw that I'd started to cry again she said, "Seriously, Millie, maybe you ought to see a doctor."

I always thought I'd be able to handle the situation with Karen better if she weren't such a mystery, so I asked Richard if I could meet her.

He said, "I hope you're joking," and I thought that was the end of it till one Sunday evening when the doorbell rang.

We'd been in the tub together and Richard's bathrobe was closest to me, so without even thinking I threw it around me and answered the door.

Our eyes met and widened and held for a long minute, and she must have been as surprised as I was to see her hair, her eyes, her mouth, her build, her stance on a stranger wearing the bathrobe she must have worn, still dripping from the bathtub where she must have bathed. Except for the ten years she had on me, we were identical.

"Hi," I said.

She looked hard at my face and then headed for her car. Her tires shrieked. I shut the door.

"Who was it?" Richard was behind me.

"I think it was Karen."

"What did she say?"

"Nothing at all."

"Did it look like Karen?"

"I don't know what Karen looks like," I said. "It looked like me."

He was putting on his coat. He was looking for his keys.

"Don't go now," I said.

"I'll be back."

"Dinner's almost ready."

"You go ahead and eat."

"I don't yell at you," I said.

"But you cry." And it was true. I was crying then.

"This is my night," I said.

He shut the door on my hand.

Casey said, "Is there some good reason you allow yourself to be treated like that?"

Chuck had finally sent word that he wasn't coming home. It was one of those postcards the hotel maid leaves in the room. On the front were pictures of a red casino, a red dining room, a red lounge.

"There must be some reason," I said.

We were sitting on the back porch, because it had the best view of the lake and the mountains behind it. Whenever I looked from that angle, I could imagine what the valley must have looked like ten thousand years ago when the lake was as big as three states back east and only the tops of the mountains poked through.

"Maybe it's the challenge," she said.

"I don't think so," I said.

"Then you tell me why."

The lake was translucent in the sunset, as if lighted from below. I imagined the capital dome sinking below the surface, the high-rises going under, the mountains shrinking down into the water.

"Do you know what he told me once?" I said. "He said if somebody was trying to kill me he'd shoot them. He said he'd shoot them even if I was only injured, if it was serious, I mean."

"Why did he say that?"

"We were arguing about gun control."

"He doesn't believe in gun control?"

"And do you know what else?" I said. "He said even if I was already dead and he knew who did it, he'd kill them. Even if I was already dead."

Casey shook her head.

"I think in Texan that means 'I love you,' " I said. "Don't you?" She rolled her eyes. "I said that if somebody was trying to hurt him I'd do anything in my power to stop them, but I didn't know if I could actually shoot somebody, I didn't know if I could shoot a gun at all."

Casey smiled at me out of her new jawline. "He's crazy not to love you," she said.

The sun fell behind some low clouds near the horizon and the lake turned dark and dull. I heard Casey groan and shift in her chair. For eight full months she had defied her condition, but in the last month she'd given in to her weariness. It was hard to see her without her strength, and harder still to realize that even at her weakest she was stronger than I'd ever be, but what was hardest, even then, was to face the truth of what she'd just said.

"Aw, Millie," she said when she looked at my face, "over a guy?" She put her arm around me and I leaned against her. Through her sweatshirt, through her skin, I could feel movement, restless and strained, a pressure that felt to me greater than anything a stomach could bear. "At least cry over something that matters."

That night Richard called and asked me to come over. When I got there he was packing. He was going with Karen to Santa Fe.

"I want you to understand that I've almost got it solved," he said. "Soon it will all be over. Then we can concentrate on us."

I went into his bathroom and locked the door. There were ten condoms in the medicine chest, five in his shaving kit, an unopened box under the sink. I opened the door. He was bent over his suitcase.

"I can't do this anymore," I said.

"I need you to be strong for two more weeks."

"You said you'd take me." His suitcase clicked shut. The phone started to ring.

"You don't own me," he said, and in that instant I could

hear the echo of him saying just those words to Karen, and to Stephanie, and to whoever came before, to every woman he'd had since he was twenty, or sixteen, or twelve. And I thought about Karen, and how Stephanie looks like us too, and I imagined five or six of us all lined up and smiling just like a family portrait to hear his forty-year refrain, the simplest answer in his clear-cut life. And I thought beyond us to all the other women who had heard those words out of other men's mouths: women with sculptured faces, with designer clothes, with graduate degrees. Women who could have any man. Women who upon hearing those words realized with something like absolute sorrow what gulf they would have to cross to be with that man. Women who started to cry, who slapped faces, who walked away. Then all the other women were gone. The phone was still ringing. I followed Richard to the garage.

"What if I ever had a real problem?" I said.

First he said, "I'd be there for you." Then he said, "Like what?"

"I don't know," I said. "What if my house burned down? What if my mother died? What if I got pregnant?"

He put down his suitcase. "Are you?" he said.

I looked into his perfect eyes. There was only one answer that would keep him from going to Santa Fe.

"Not to the best of my knowledge," I said.

"Well, if you were," he said, "then we'd get married and have a family." He threw his suitcase in the trunk, closed the car door, and drove away.

I got in my car and drove straight to the lake and across what was left of the parking lot. I put my front tires in the water. I wondered how deep the water got between me and the island, and I wondered if my car would float, and I wondered what people thought about right before they decided not to live anymore, and then I thought about the perfect tightness of Casey's stomach. The wind rose out of the west and I could hear tiny waves lapping around my tires. I backed the car up a few feet, crawled into the backseat, and went to sleep.

I woke up in the middle of a lightning storm. By the look of the light it was midafternoon. There were two-foot waves all across the lake, and I could feel them splash against the underside of the car. I started it up and got back on the highway. When I pulled into my driveway, Casey's car was gone.

By the time I got to room 427 I was afraid to knock on the door. I went back to the lobby and bought a white calla lily for Casey because it looked both sexy and pure, and I bought the biggest stuffed animal in the gift store, a moose with red ribbon in his horns. I bought magazines for Casey and some candy in case she was hungry, and then I was out of money, and I had to go back upstairs. I stood in front of her door for ten minutes before a nurse came by and asked if she could help me.

"Do you know if she's awake?" I said. "I thought she might be sleeping."

"Go on in," the nurse said. "She's trying to feed her baby."

Against the steel-gray curtains, against the steel-gray afternoon, against the metallic machines that kept track of her, Casey was warm and amber and serene. She smiled at me and my lily and my moose and my magazines. She held out her hand. Under her other arm was the baby.

"Look at his fingers" was the first thing she said. I had to unwrap the blanket to see them. I had to lift the small pink arm, unfold it from itself. His fingers were almost as long as his forearm. When he grabbed my thumb, they wrapped all the way around.

There was a big white clip on his belly button.

"Do you think that would make a noise if someone tried to take him out of the hospital?" Casey said. "Do you think that's what it's for?"

I shrugged, and realized I hadn't said anything.

"Hold him, Millie," she said.

I lifted him out of the nest her arm had made. He didn't open his eyes, but it was clear he wanted to stay. I rocked him and walked towards the window. The gray was getting darker. The wind was picking up.

"Did it hurt bad?"

"More than you could ever imagine," she said. "More than you could ever prepare yourself for. It's not like cramps, Millie. It's nothing like cramps."

I steadied myself on the windowsill.

"He ripped me open, coming out. They had to sew me up."

For a second I was afraid I might faint and drop the baby. Casey's eyes showed nothing but peace.

"Frankly, I can't imagine anyone having two kids," she said, "anyone being willing to go through this more than once. I can't believe my mother did this. My mother did this four times."

"I'm sorry I wasn't here, Casey. I'm sorry I wasn't near a phone."

"I kind of wanted to do it alone," she said. "I did it. It's done."

Way to the west, across the valley and over the lake, a sliver of sun was hitting the top of Antelope Island, and I wondered if there were any antelope out there, if they understood the limitations of the island they were trapped on. I wondered what would happen to them if the lake continued to rise, if they would move up with the level of the lake, or if they would consider diving in and setting out across all that cold dead water.

At least two hours a day, I had told the doctor when she asked me how much I was crying, and then she had raised her eyebrows, and then she had written the prescription I hadn't filled.

And I looked again at the baby's long red fingers and imagined some younger version of myself, of Casey, telling the face that would one day be connected to them: "You have great beauty and grace." And I thought about the passion those fingers might raise and the helpless way the young man who would own them might look at his hands because he couldn't find answers to the questions that the young woman he couldn't help hurting was born knowing there weren't any answers for.

"I wish Chuck could see him," Casey said, in a voice that was small but not sad, and I wondered how two men who at one time seemed so different could have turned out, in the end, to be exactly the same.

I looked hard at her face to try and understand her pain, to try and make up for what I had missed because of my pain, which was so awfully small, to tap into her calm, to appropriate it somehow. But it wasn't the face I remembered. Everything about it had changed.

"It's okay," she said, and reached her arms toward her baby. And I imagined myself running with him out the hospital doors, the clip on his belly beeping wildly, and I wondered about people who wanted babies to fill spaces in their lives and I knew it wouldn't work for me because I'd been taught to believe that some spaces you just can't fill. And when I handed Casey back her baby, when our hands touched underneath his back, I realized I didn't feel like crying anymore. And as I watched her tuck him back under her arm, watched her tuck the edge of the blanket under each set of those newborn piano fingers, I was breathless and frightened by the frailty of miracles, and full of the fact of our lives.

For Bo

--- --- --- --- --- --- --- --- ---

When we come home from the regular Friday-night parties, my husband, Sam, plays guitar for the dogs. They sit next to him on the couch, one on either side, press their heads against his thighs, and wag their tails. He sings every song ever written with "dog" in the title, and then improvises by substituting dog-words for people-words: "You Are the Canine of My Life," or "Born to Bark." He can keep it up for hours, and the dogs never get tired of listening. Usually I find him asleep there the next morning, with the dogs piled on top of him and his guitar propped up against the coffee table.

Every Saturday morning, at eight a.m. my time, my mother calls to ask me if I am pregnant. Her greatest fear is that I'll start having babies before I finish becoming successful. I come from a long line of successful women, and I know I keep her awake at night with worry. It would greatly ease her mind to know that my husband had a vasectomy years before I met him, but withholding this information from her makes me feel a little powerful.

My mother doesn't really like my husband. I don't think she's had much interaction with tattooed people. When we go to Pennsylvania to visit my parents, they rent a house in New Jersey—where they don't know anyone—and we can all lose ourselves in the tan and blondness of the beach. We don't go there often anymore, and my mother blames the dogs.

"Those dogs have taken you right out of my life," she said, one Saturday, long-distance. She doesn't even know about the horse.

"We might make it out in September," I told her.

"Oh good," she said. "Rentals are cheap then."

My mother worries constantly, but she doesn't perspire or grow body hair. She is absolutely sure that I am dying of a venereal disease I contracted from my husband.

"He's just not sanitary," she said. "Those tattoos . . . and those great big dogs. You know I don't even go into Jacuzzis anymore. And I haven't used a public rest room in years." Somewhere inside my mother's body there is a reservoir nearly full of sweat, hair, and other restrained excretions.

"I'm sending you some hot curlers, and a wonderful new apricot scrub," she said. "Do you have *any* new spring clothes at all?"

My mother is certain that my becoming successful depends upon the curl of my hair and the absence of blemishes on my face.

"What you really need," she said, "is a slim white purse."

The clock by the bed says eight twenty-five, and I stretch and remember why my mother hasn't called. She's flying to San Francisco today on business, and she's managed a three-hour layover here in Denver so we can have dinner and visit.

I hear Sam's circular saw in the backyard. He's enlarging the deck, making room for the new addition.

"No dog of mine," he says, "is going to have to lay around in the dirt."

The first Saturday in May is more than just Kentucky Derby Day at our house. Each year since we've been married we watch the Derby, get a little stupid on Kentucky bourbon, and head for the dog pound. It's become a three-year tradition, and if we hadn't lost Hazel to cancer last winter, we'd be going on dog number four.

Another tradition in our house is to spend at least half of every weekend in bed, and Sam finishes the porch and joins me under the covers. Sam says our gravestones will read: "They never had a lot of money, but they always had a lot of sex." You can probably understand why my mother doesn't like Sam. She gets most of her information from my Aunt Colleen, who moved out here several years ago. Colleen's got lots of money and very little imagination. Last time they talked, she told my mother that one of these days I would wake up and realize that squalor is not enough, and now my mother is holding her breath. Colleen's an attractive woman for her age, but her hair is always stiff, and a lot of her clothes have comic-strip characters printed on them. Sam says she shouldn't knock squalor till she's tried it.

I've invited Colleen to dinner today too. Sam thinks I'm asking for trouble, but I try to do what I can for my family. Besides, Colleen offered to drive my mother to and from the airport, which means I won't have to watch her cry.

We wake up sticky and lazy and fight each other for the first shower. I drip through the kitchen and crack eggs into the cast-iron skillet. I cook enough sausage for all of us, and the dogs sit patiently at my feet.

Sam has been admiring himself in the mirror for several minutes. It's finally warm enough for him to wear his new swim trunks. They are sky-blue with pink sharks swimming in every direction across them. The sharks are smiling, and wearing black sunglasses.

"I am one handsome motherfucker," he tells his reflection.

I go to my closet and choose a denim skirt my mother sent me, and a dark blouse that I think makes me look thin and neat. Sam whistles long and clear. The dogs come running.

"George, Graci, come on in here and take a look at your sexy mom," he says. Graci licks my knees.

Our yard is full of wild mint, and I'm mixing juleps for the Derby. Our blender is broken and the drinks taste like bourbon on the rocks, but we swallow whole mugfuls while the TV sings "My Old Kentucky Home." The jockeys, sitting atop horses no bigger than dogs, are locked one slam at a time into the metal starting gate. The front gates open and the horses race forward, silks shining in the sun.

The even-money horse pulls up around the first turn, blood pouring from his nostrils. He's loaded into an ambulance before the other horses turn for home.

"God would have never made an animal that frail," Sam says.

The horse that wins pays 15–1 odds, and it's the jockey's birthday so we are happy for him.

"What luck," Sam says, "to be born so short on Kentucky Derby Day."

There is a knock at the door and I see Colleen's red Corvette out the window, still running. I open the door to hugs and kisses out of the side of my mother's mouth.

"Are we early?" my mother says, looking at my untucked shirt.

"No, no. Come in," I say.

"Do you think we could rearrange the cars, dear?" Colleen says. "I don't want to park on the street in this neighborhood."

I pull our pickup truck out of the driveway and park it on the street. I get out and my mother hugs me again.

"*This* is the brand-new truck?" she asks, over my shoulder. The paint in the bed is already scratched—in some places down to the primer. Muddy cat paws dot the hood.

"Nothing like a pickup for carting the family around," Sam says, from the front door. George shoots between his legs and I watch wet paws collide with the pink serge of Colleen's skirt.

"Let's all go inside," I say. "Honey, maybe you should put the dogs out back." Sam raises his eyebrows.

"Please," I say.

He slinks to the back door and the dogs follow, tails between legs.

"That's not the skirt I sent you?" my mother asks.

I nod.

"Sweetheart," she says, "if you don't tuck in the blouse it looks like some kind of an old rag." She has unzipped my skirt and is furiously tucking in my shirt. Long coral nails catch my skin.

"Now, do you have a contour belt?"

It sounds geologic. I shake my head.

"I've got one you can have," Colleen says. "It's way too big for me."

Now my mother is pulling my shirt back out of my skirt. She ties it in a knot at my waist.

"That'll do for now," she says.

I hear Sam coming through the kitchen. "Hey," he says, "I think my wife's old enough to dress herself, what do you think, Colleen?"

"I'd think so," Colleen says.

"You would think so, wouldn't you?" my mother says. She takes a comb out of her purse and teases my hair in front.

"You know it's just because I adore you," she says.

I pull gently away and move toward the kitchen

"I thought I'd make a salad," I say. Salad is a safe bet with people like Colleen and my mother, who eat cocktail onions for their nutritional value.

"Anybody need a mint julep?" Sam asks.

Wide World of Sports is now covering a weightlifting competition in Hawaii. Colleen is mesmerized, and I watch her lip curl into a sneer of desire and disgust.

"Don't you have any vodka?" my mother asks.

I stand in the kitchen scrubbing vegetables with all my might. I've spent half our grocery allowance on specialty foods for this salad: artichoke hearts, crabmeat, feta cheese, imported Greek olives.

Sam makes another mint julep for himself and two vodkas on the rocks for Colleen and my mother. The dogs scratch and whine at the back door. Sam moves to open it.

"They'll be good," he says.

George runs straight to my mother and drops a soggy tennis ball between her knees. Graci runs to Colleen, who screams at her to sit. Graci sits on Colleen's feet and I see a thin yellow trickle emerge between her Gucci sandals.

"It's a mistake to yell at Graci," Sam says. "Her bladder's undersized."

"Everyone come and eat," I say.

The four of us sit around the wooden table Sam made with two-by-fours and sixteen-penny nails. Graci is curled under my chair, and it wobbles when she breathes. I see George's head on Sam's lap.

"Great-looking salad, lamb-cakes," Sam says.

"Glorious," says my mother. "I never spring for crabmeat . . . or is this imitation?"

"No, no. It's real," I say. I sneak a piece of feta cheese to Graci. "My pay raise just went into effect."

"You got a raise?" Colleen asks.

I nod.

"That's wonderful, darling," my mother says. "Do you know that your complexion is looking the very best I've ever seen it?"

"It must be the dry air," Colleen says.

"And the apricot scrub," I say. "The apricot scrub is great."

"Why, it's so great," Sam says, "that I've been spreadin' it on toast." I watch him eat carefully around the green peas on his plate.

"Who says salads aren't filling?" My mother stands and moves toward the window. "I have some curtains that would really work here," she says. "I'll mail them to you when I get home if you promise to put them up."

I nod.

"You promise, really?"

I nod again.

Sam says, "Would you look at what time it's gettin' to be."

We stand in the doorway and wave as Colleen and my mother drive away. I feel light-headed and move toward the bedroom. Sam catches my arm.

"The pound closes in forty-five minutes," he says.

I pull the truck up in front of the huge iron gates, and Sam is out the door before I set the parking brake. We are fifty yards from the building and already we can hear the barking.

"You lose your dog?" a smiling gray-haired man in a police uniform shouts over the ruckus.

"No. We want to adopt one," Sam says.

"Take a look," he shouts, indicating an iron-barred door. "The ones with the yellow tags are ready to go. Keep your hands away from the biters."

When we enter the long gray corridor the dogs give new meaning to the word "deafening." There must be fifty of them, each straining to be heard above the rest. Before we get halfway down the aisle I see the dog Sam will choose. A mottled, long-eared houndish creature with paws the size of grapefruits, one brown eye and one blue.

"Nice-lookin' dog," he says when we get to the cage.

It's easily the ugliest dog I've ever seen in my life.

"I think he likes you," I say. The blue eye seems to follow Sam down the corridor, while the brown one stays fixed on me.

"He's the one," Sam says. "We'll call him Arlo."

There is another crescendo of barking as Arlo's cage is opened and he races out into the corridor.

Sam holds Arlo's back end on his lap while Arlo eats orange peels off the floor of the truck. We stop in the park to let him run around——get acquainted with us before he meets the other dogs. After two bags of potato chips he almost knows how to sit.

"He's gonna be a smart one," Sam says.

The sun is low and orange in the sky, and the branches of the young cherry trees are bent almost to breaking with blossoms.

"Next year we'll have a girl," Sam says. "Something smaller that won't eat so much. After that we'll probably have to move out to the country."

"Or stop getting dogs," I say.

Sam's face clouds with the mistrust he reserves for Colleen and my mother.

"It's bad luck to break a tradition," he says. He stands up and pulls on my hand. "We better get home and get back into bed."

What Shock Heard

I t was late spring, but the dry winds had started already, and we were trying to load Shock into the horse trailer for a trip to the vet and the third set of X-rays on her fetlock. She's just barely green broke, and after months of being lame she was hot as a pistol and not willing to come within twenty yards of the trailer. Katie and Irwin, who own the barn, and know a lot more than me, had lip chains out, and lunge ropes and tranquilizer guns, but for all their contraptions they couldn't even get close enough to her to give her the shot. Crazy Billy was there too, screaming about two-by-fours and electric prods, and women being too damned ignorant to train a horse right. His horses would stand while he somersaulted in and out of the saddle. They'd stand where he ground-tied them, two feet from the train tracks, one foot off the highway. He lost a horse under a semi once, and almost killed the driver. All the women were afraid of him, and the cowboys said he trained with Quaaludes. I was watching him close, trying to be patient with Katie and Irwin and my brat of a horse, but I didn't want Billy within ten feet of Shock, no matter how long it took to get her in the trailer.

That's when the new cowboy walked up, like out of nowhere with a carrot in his hands, whispered something in Shock's ear, and she walked right behind him into the trailer. He winked at me and I smiled back and poor Irwin and Katie were just standing there all tied up in their own whips and chains.

The cowboy walked on into the barn then, and I got into the truck with Katie and Irwin and didn't see him again for two months when Shock finally got sound and I was starting to ride her in short sessions and trying to teach her some of the things any five-year-old horse should know.

It was the middle of prairie summer by then and it was brutal just thinking about putting on long pants to ride, but I went off Shock so often I had to. The cowboy told me his name was Zeke, short for Ezekiel, and I asked him if he was religious and he said only about certain things.

I said my name was Raye, and he said that was his mother's name and her twin sister's name was Faye, and I said I could never understand why people did things like that to their children. I said that I was developing a theory that what people called you had everything to do with the person you turned out to become, and he said he doubted it 'cause that was just words, and was I going to stand there all day or was I going to come riding with him. He winked at Billy then and Billy grinned and I pretended not to see and hoped to myself that they weren't the same kind of asshole.

I knew Shock wasn't really up to the kind of riding I'd have to do to impress this cowboy, but it had been so long since I'd been out on the meadows I couldn't say no. There was something about the prairie for me—it wasn't where I had come from, but when I moved there it just took me in and I knew I couldn't ever stop living under that big sky. When I was a little girl driving with my family from our cabin in Montana across Nebraska to all the grandparents in Illinois, I used to be scared of the flatness because I didn't know what was holding all the air in.

Some people have such a fear of the prairie it makes them crazy, my ex-husband was one, and they even have a word for it: "agoraphobia." But when I looked it up in Greek it said "fear of the marketplace," and that seems like the opposite kind of fear to me. He was afraid of the high wind and the big storms that never even came while he was alive. When he shot himself, people said it was my fault for making him move here and making him stay, but his chart only said *acute agoraphobia* and I think he did it because his life wasn't as much like a book as he wanted it to be. He taught me about literature and language, and even though he used language in a bad way—to make up worlds that hurt us—I learned about its power and it got me a job, if nothing else, writing for enough money to pay off his debts.

But I wasn't thinking about any of that when I set off across the meadow at an easy hand gallop behind Zeke and his gelding Jesse. The sun was low in the sky, but it wasn't too long after solstice and in the summer the sun never seemed to fall, it seeped toward the horizon and then melted into it. The fields were losing heat, though, and at that pace we could feel the bands of warmth and cool coming out of the earth like it was some perfectly regulated machine. I could tell Zeke wasn't a talker, so I didn't bother riding up with him; I didn't want Shock to try and race on her leg. I hung back and

watched the way his body moved with the big quarter horse:
brown skin stretched across muscle and horseflesh, black
mane and sandy hair, breath and sweat and one dust cloud
rose around them till there was no way to separate the rider
from the ride.

Zeke was a hunter. He made his living as a hunter's guide,
in Alaska, in places so remote, he said, that the presence of
one man with a gun was insignificant. He invited me home for
moose steaks, and partly because I loved the way the two
words sounded together, I accepted.

It was my first date in almost six years and once I got that
into my head it wouldn't leave me alone. It had been almost
two years since I'd been with a man, two years almost to the
day that Charlie sat on our front-porch swing and blew his
brains out with a gun so big the stains splattered three sets of
windows and even wrapped around the corner of the house. I
thought I had enough reason to swear off men for a while, and
Charlie wasn't in the ground three months when I got another
one.

It was in October of that same year, already cold and getting dark too early, and Shock and I got back to the barn
about an hour after sunset. Katie and Irwin were either in
town or in bed and the barn was as dark as the house. I
walked Shock into her stall and was starting to take off her
saddle when Billy stepped out of the shadows with a shoeing
tool in his hand. Women always say they know when it's
going to happen, and I did, as soon as he slid the stall door
open. I went down when the metal hit my shoulder and I
couldn't see anything but I could feel his body shuddering
already and little flecks of spit coming out of his mouth. The
straw wasn't clean and Shock was nervous and I concentrated

on the sound her hooves made as they snapped the air searchingly behind her. I imagined them connecting with Billy's skull and how the blood on the white wall would look like Charlie's, but Shock was much too honest a horse to aim for impact. Billy had the arm that wasn't numb pinned down with one knee through the whole thing, but I bit him once right on the jawline and he's still got that scar; a half-moon of my teeth in his face.

He said he'd kill me if I told, and the way my life was going it seemed reasonable to take him at his word. I had a hard time getting excited about meeting men after that. I'd learned to live without it, but not very well.

Shock had pitched me over her head twice the day that Zeke asked me to dinner, and by the time I got to his house my neck was so stiff I had to turn my whole body to look at him.

"Why don't you just jump in the hot tub before dinner," he said, and I swung my head and shoulders around from him to the wood-heated hot tub in the middle of the living room and I must have gone real white then because he said, "But you know, the heater's messing up and it's just not getting as hot as it should."

While he went outside to light the charcoals I sat on a hard wooden bench covered with skins facing what he called the trophy wall. A brown-and-white speckled owl stared down its pointed beak at me from above the doorway, its wings and talons poised as if ready for attack, a violence in its huge yellow eyes that is never so complete in humans.

He came back in and caught me staring into the face of the grizzly bear that covered most of the wall. "It's an eight-foot-square bear," he said, and then explained, by rubbing his hand across the fur, that it was eight feet long from the tip of its nose to the tip of its tail, and from the razor edge of one outstretched front claw to the other. He smoothed the fur back down with strong even strokes. He picked something off one of its teeth.

"It's a decent-sized bear," he said, "but they get much bigger."

I told him about the time I was walking with my dogs along the Salmon River and I saw a deer carcass lying in the middle of an active spawning ground. The salmon were deeper than the water and their tails slapped the surface as they clustered around the deer. One dog ran in to chase them, and they didn't even notice, they swam around her ankles till she got scared and came out.

He laughed and reached towards me and I thought *for* me, but then his hand came down on the neck of a six-point mule deer mounted on the wall behind me. "Isn't he beautiful?" he asked. His hands rubbed the short hair around the deer's ears. It was hanging closer to me than I realized, and when I touched its nose it was warmer than my hands.

He went back outside then and I tried to think of more stories to tell him but I got nervous all over and started fidgeting with something that I realized too late was the foot of a small furry animal. The thing I was sitting on reminded me a little too much of my dog to allow me to relax.

The moose steaks were lean and tender and it was easy to eat them until he started telling me about their history, about the bull that had come to the clearing for water, and had seen Zeke there, had seen the gun even, and trusted him not to fire. I couldn't look right at him then, and he waited awhile and he said, "Do you have any idea what they do to cows?"

We talked about other things after that, horses and the prairie and the mountains we had both left for it. At two I said I should go home, and he said he was too tired to take me. I wanted him to touch me the way he touched the mule deer but he threw a blanket over me and told me to lift up for the pillow. Then he climbed up and into a loft I hadn't even noticed, and left me down there in the dark under all those frightened eyes.

The most remarkable thing about him, I guess, was his calm: His hands were quieter on Jesse's mane even than mine were on Shock's. I never heard him raise his voice, even in laughter. There wasn't an animal in the barn he couldn't turn to putty, and I knew it must be the same with the ones he shot.

On our second ride he talked more, even about himself some, horses he'd sold, and ex-lovers; there was a darkness in him I couldn't locate.

It was the hottest day of that summer and it wouldn't have been right to run the horses, so we let them walk along the creek bank all afternoon, clear into the next county, I think.

He asked me why I didn't move to the city, why I hadn't, at least, while Charlie was sick, and I wondered what version of my life he had heard. I told him I needed the emptiness and the grasses and the storm threats. I told him about my job and the articles I was working on and how I knew if I moved to the city, or the ocean, or even back to the mountains, I'd be paralyzed. I told him that it seemed as if the right words could only come to me out of the perfect semicircular space of the prairie.

He rubbed his hands together fist to palm and smiled, and asked if I wanted to rest. He said he might nap, if it was quiet, and I said I knew I always talked too much, and he said it was okay because I didn't mind if he didn't always listen.

I told him words were all we had, something that Charlie had told me, and something I had believed because it let me fall into a vacuum where I didn't have to justify my life.

Zeke was stretching his neck in a funny way, so without asking I went over and gave him a back rub and when I was finished he said, "For a writer lady you do some pretty good communicating without words," but he didn't touch me even then, and I sat very still while the sun melted, embarrassed and afraid to even look at him.

Finally, he stood up and stretched.

"Billy says you two go out sometimes."

"Billy lies," I said.

"He knows a lot about you," he said.

"No more than everyone else in town," I said. "People talk. It's just what they do. I'll tell you all about it if you want to know."

"We're a long way from the barn," he said, in a way that I couldn't tell if it was good or bad. He was rubbing one palm against the other so slowly it was making my skin crawl.

"Shock's got good night vision," I said, as evenly as I could.

He reached for a strand of Shock's mane and she rubbed her whole neck against him. I pulled her forelock out from under the brow band. She nosed his back pockets, where the carrots were. She knocked his cap off his head and scratched her nose between his shoulder blades. He put both hands up on her withers and rubbed little circles. She stretched her neck out long and low.

"Your horse is a whore, Raye," he said.

"I want to know what you said to her to make her follow you into the trailer," I said.

"What I said to her?" he said. "Christ, Raye, there aren't
any words for that."

Then he was up and in the saddle and waiting for me to get
back on Shock. He took off when I had only one foot in the
stirrup, and I just hung around Shock's neck for the first
quarter mile till he slowed up.

The creek trail was narrow and Shock wanted to race, so I
got my stirrup and let her fly past him on the outside, the
wheat so high it whipped across Shock's shoulder and my
thigh. Once we were in the lead, Shock really turned it on and
I could feel her strength and the give of her muscles and the
solidity of the healed fetlock every time it hit the ground.
Then I heard Jesse coming on the creek side, right at Shock's
flank, and I knew we were coming to the big ditch, and I knew
Shock would take it if Jesse did, but neither of us wanted to
give up the lead. Shock hit the edge first and sailed over it and
I came way up on her neck and held my breath when her front
legs hit, but then we were down on the other side and she was
just as strong and as sound as ever. Jesse edged up again and I
knew we couldn't hold the lead for much longer. I felt Zeke's
boots on my calf and our stirrups locked once for an instant
and then he pulled away. I let Shock slow then, and when
Jesse's dust cleared, the darkening sky opened around me
like an invitation.

It wasn't light enough to run anymore and we were still ten
miles from the barn. Jupiter was up, and Mars. There wasn't
any moon.

Zeke said, "Watching you ride made me almost forget to
beat you." I couldn't see his face in the shadows.

He wanted silence but it was too dark not to talk, so I
showed him the constellations. I told him the stories I knew
about them: Cassiopeia weeping on the King's shoulder while

the great winged Pegasus carries her daughter off across the eastern sky. Cygnus, the swan, flying south along the milky way, the Great Bear spinning slowly head over tail in the north. I showed him Andromeda, the galaxy closest to our own. I said, "It's two hundred million light-years away. Do you know what that means?" And when he didn't answer I said, "It means the light we see left that galaxy two hundred million years ago." And then I said, "Doesn't that make you feel insignificant?"

And he said, "No."

"How does it make you feel?" I said.

"Like I've gotten something I might not deserve," he said.

Then he went away hunting in Montana for six weeks. I kept thinking about him up there in the mountains I had come from and wondering if he saw them the way I did, if he saw how they held the air. He didn't write or call once, and I didn't either, because I thought I was being tested and I wanted to pass. He left me a key so I could water his plants and keep chemicals in his hot tub. I got friendly with the animals on the wall, and even talked to them sometimes, like I did to the plants. The only one I avoided was the Dall sheep. Perfect in its whiteness, and with a face as gentle and wise as Buddha. I didn't want to imagine Zeke's hands pulling the trigger that stained the white neck with blood the taxidermist must have struggled to remove.

He asked me to keep Jesse in shape for him too, and I did. I'd work Shock in the ring for an hour and then take Jesse out on the trails. He was a little nervous around me, being used to Zeke's uncanny calm, I guess, so I sang the songs to him that I remembered from Zeke's records: "Angel from Montgomery," "City of New Orleans," "L.A. Freeway," places I'd never been or cared to go. I didn't know any songs about Montana.

When we'd get back to the barn I'd brush Jesse till he shone, rubbing around his face and ears with a chamois cloth till he finally let down his guard a little and leaned into my hands. I fed him boxes full of carrots while Shock looked a question at me out of the corner of her eye.

One night Jesse and I got back late from a ride and the only car left at the barn was Billy's. I walked Jesse up and down the road twice before I thought to look in Zeke's saddlebags for the hunting knife I should have known would be there all along. I put it in the inside pocket of my jean jacket and felt powerful, even though I hadn't thought ahead as far as using it. When I walked through the barn door I hit the breaker switch that turned on every light and there was Billy leaning against the door to Jesse's stall.

"So now she's riding his horse," he said.

"You want to open that door?" I said. I stood as tall as I could between him and Jesse.

"Does that mean you're going steady?"

"Let me by," I said.

"It'd be a shame if he came back and there wasn't any horse to ride," he said, and I grabbed for Jesse's reins but he moved forward faster, spooking Jesse, who reared and spun and clattered out the open barn door. I listened to his hooves on the stone and then outside on the hard dirt till he got so far away I only imagined it.

Billy shoved me backwards into a wheelbarrow and when my head hit the manure I reached for the knife and got it between us and he took a step backwards and wiped the spit off his mouth.

"You weren't that much fun the first time," he said, and

ran for the door. I heard him get into his car and screech out the driveway, and I lay there in the manure, breathing horse piss and praying he wouldn't hit Jesse out on the hard road. I got up slow and went into the tack room for a towel and I tried to clean my hair with it but it was Zeke's and it smelled like him and I couldn't understand why my timing had been so bad all my life. I wrapped my face in it so tight I could barely breathe and sat on his tack box and leaned into the wall, but then I remembered Jesse and put some grain in a bucket and went out into the darkness and whistled.

It was late September and almost midnight and all the stars I'd shown Zeke had shifted a half turn to the west. Orion was on the horizon, his bow drawn back, aimed across the Milky Way at the Great Bear, I guess, if space curves the way Earth does. Jesse wasn't anywhere, and I walked half the night looking for him. I went to sleep in my truck and at dawn Irwin and Jesse showed up at the barn door together.

"He got spooked," I told Irwin. "I was too worried to go home."

Irwin looked hard at me. "Hear anything from Zeke?" he said.

I spent a lot of time imagining his homecoming. I'd make up the kind of scenes in my head I knew would never happen, the kind that never happen to anyone, where the man gets out of the car so fast he tears his jacket, and when he lifts the woman up against the sky she is so light that she thinks she may be absorbed into the atmosphere.

I had just come back from a four-hour ride when his truck did pull up to the barn, six weeks to the day from when he left. He got out slow as ever, and then went around back to where he kept his carrots. From the tack-room window I watched him rub Jesse and feed him, pick up one of his front hooves, run his fingers through his tail.

I wanted to look busy but I'd just got done putting everything away so I sat on the floor and started oiling my tack and then wished I hadn't because of what I'd smell like when he saw me. It was fifteen minutes before he even came looking, and I had the bridle apart, giving it the oil job of its life. He put his hands on the doorjamb and smiled big.

"Put that thing back together and come riding with me," he said.

"I just got back," I said. "Jesse and I've been all over."

"That'll make it easier for you to beat me on your horse," he said. "Come on, it's getting dark earlier every night."

He stepped over me and pulled his saddle off the rack, and I put the bridle back together as fast as I could. He was still ready before I was and he stood real close while I tried to make Shock behave and get tacked up and tried not to let my hands shake when I fastened the buckles.

Then we were out in the late sunshine and it was like he'd never left, except this time he was galloping before he hit the end of the driveway.

"Let's see that horse run," he called to me, and Jesse shot across the road and the creek trail and plunged right through the middle of the wheat field. The wheat was so tall I could barely see Zeke's head, but the footing was good and Shock was gaining on him. I thought about the farmer who'd shoot us if he saw us, and I thought about all the hours I'd spent on Jesse keeping him in shape so that Zeke could come home and win another race. The sky was black to the west and coming in fast, and I tried to remember if I'd heard a forecast and to feel if there was any direction to the wind. Then we were out in a hay field that had just been cut and rolled, and it smelled so strong and sweet it made me light-headed and I thought maybe we weren't touching ground at all but flying along above it, buoyed up by the fragrance and the swirl of the wind. I drove Shock straight at a couple of bales that were tied together and made her take them, and she did, but by the time we hit the irrigation ditch we'd lost another couple of seconds on Zeke.

I felt the first drops of rain and tried to yell up to Zeke, but the wind came up suddenly and blasted my voice back into my mouth. I knew there was no chance of catching him then, but I dug my heels in and yipped a little and Shock dug in even harder, but then I felt her front hoof hit a gopher hole and the bottom dropped out and she went down and I went forward over her neck and then she came down over me. My face hit first and I tasted blood and a hoof came down on the back of my head and I heard reins snap and waited for another hoof to hit, but then it was quiet and I knew she had cleared me. At least I'm not dead, I thought, but my head hurt too bad to even move.

I felt the grit inside my mouth and thought of Zeke galloping on across the prairie, enclosed in the motion, oblivious to my fall. It would be a mile, maybe two, before he slowed down and looked behind him, another before he'd stop, aware of my absence, and come back for me.

I opened one eye and saw Shock grazing nearby, broken reins hanging uneven below her belly. If she'd re-pulled the tendon in her fetlock it would be weeks, maybe months, before I could ride with him again. My mouth was full of blood and my lips were swelling so much it was running out the sides, though I kept my jaw clamped and my head down. The wind was coming in little gusts now, interrupted by longer and longer periods of calm, but the sky was getting darker

and I lifted my head to look for Zeke. I got dizzy, and I closed
my eyes and tried to breathe regularly. In what seemed like a
long time I started to hear a rhythm in my head and I pressed
my ear into the dust and knew it was Zeke coming back across
the field at a gallop, balanced and steady, around the holes
and over them. Then I heard his boots hit ground. He tied
Jesse first, and then caught Shock, which was smart, I guess,
and then he knelt next to my head and I opened the eye that
wasn't in the dirt and he smiled and put his hands on his
knees.

"Your mouth," he said, without laughing, but I knew what
I must've looked like, so I raised up on one elbow and started
to tell him I was okay and he said,

"Don't talk. It'll hurt."

And he was right, it did, but I kept on talking and soon I
was telling him about the pain in my mouth and the back of
my head and what Billy had done that day in the barn, and the
ghosts I carry with me. Blood was coming out with the words
and pieces of tooth, and I kept talking till I told him everything, but when I looked at his face I knew all I'd done was
make the gap wider with the words I'd picked so carefully
that he didn't want to hear. The wind started up again and the
rain was getting steady.

I was crying then, but not hard, and you couldn't tell
through all the dirt and blood, and the rain and the noise the
wind was making. I was crying, I think, but I wanted to laugh
because he would have said there weren't any words for what
I didn't tell him, and that was that I loved him and even more
I loved the prairie that wouldn't let you hide anything, even if
you wanted to.

Then he reached across the space my words had made
around me and put his long brown finger against my swollen

lips. I closed my eyes tight as his hand wrapped up my jaw
and I fell into his chest and whatever it was that drove him to
me, and I held myself there unbreathing, like waiting for the
sound of hooves on the sand, like waiting for a tornado.

Dall

I am not a violent person. I don't shoot animals and I hate cold weather, so maybe I had no business following Boone to the Alaska Range for a season of Dall sheep hunting. But right from the beginning, my love for Boone was a little less like contentment and a little more like sickness, so when he said he needed an assistant guide I bought a down coat and packed my bags. I had an idea about Alaska: that the wildness of the place would enlarge my range of possibility. The northern lights, for example, were something I wanted to see.

After the first week in Alaska I began to realize that the object of sheep hunting was to intentionally deprive yourself of all the comforts of normal life. We would get up at three a.m., and leave the cabin, knowing it would be nearly twenty-four hours, if not several days, before we would return. Everything depended upon the sheep, where they were and how far we could chase them. Boone was a hunter of the everything-has-to-be-hard-and-painful-to-be-good variety, and there was nothing he liked better than a six- or seven-hour belly crawl through the soggy green tundra.

The weather was almost always bad. If it wasn't raining, it was sleeting or snowing. If the sun came out, the wind started to blow. We carried heavy packs full of dry and warm clothing, but if we saw some sheep and started stalking them, we had to leave our packs behind so that we'd be less conspicuous, and often we didn't return to them until after dark. We got our feet wet very early in the day. We carried only enough water so that we were always on the edge of real thirst. We ate Spam for lunch every day, even though smoked baby clams and dried fruit would have weighed considerably less in our backpacks. It seemed important, in fact, not to eat any fruits and vegetables, to climb up and down the steepest part of every mountain, and to nearly always get caught out after dark.

Boone and I were a good team, except when we fell into one of our fights, which were infrequent but spectacular. In Alaska we seemed to fight every time we had a minute alone, and those minutes were rare with a series of hunters who were scared of the bears and half in love with Boone's macho besides.

When Boone got really mad at me, when his face puffed up and his temples bulged out and he talked through his teeth and little flecks of spit splattered my face, it was so comic and so different from his guidely calm that I was always waiting for him to laugh, like it was all a big joke that I hadn't quite gotten. And when he grabbed me so hard he made me yell or threw me on the bed or kicked my legs out from under me it always felt less like violence and more like a pratfall. Like we were acting out a scene, waiting for some signal from the audience that the absurdity of Boone's actions had been properly conveyed.

Several times in my life I've sat with women, friends of mine, who reveal, sometimes shyly, sometimes proudly, bruises of one kind or another, and I know I've said, "If it happens one time, leave him," I've said, "It doesn't matter how much you love him. Leave him if it happens one time." And I've said it with utter confidence, as if I knew what the hell I was talking about, as if violence was something that could be easily defined.

It was never that clear-cut with Boone and me. For all the shoving around he did, he never hit me, never hurt me really. I'm big and strong and always tan, so I don't bruise easily. And I was always touched, in some strange way, by the ambivalence of his violent acts; they were at once aggressive and protective, as if he wanted not to hurt me but just to contain me, as if he wanted not to break me but just to shut me off.

We took four hunters out that season, one at a time for fourteen days each, and gave them the workout of their lives. We hiked on an average of fifteen miles a day, with a vertical gain of between four and five thousand feet; roughly equivalent to hiking in and out of the Grand Canyon every day for two months. At first confused by my presence and ability, the hunters would learn fast that I was their only ally, the one who would slip them extra candy bars, the one they could whine to.

"Aren't you hungry?" they'd whisper to me when Boone was out of earshot.

And I'd say, "How about a little lunch, Boone?" and Boone would look at me exasperated.

"We're hunting, baby," he'd say, as if that explained everything. "We'll eat as soon as we can."

We did the dishes with stream water that had so much silt in it that they looked muddier every time we washed them. The cabin was only eight by ten and we took turns standing in the center of the floor over the washbasin to brush our teeth, and then one at a time we got ready for bed. Two half-cots/half-hammocks folded out of the wall into something like bunk beds. The hunter slept in the top bunk and I got the bottom. Boone spread his ground pad and sleeping bag on what was left of the floor.

Every night we'd wait until the hunter started to snore and then Boone would climb into my bunk and we'd make slow and utterly silent love. There was barely enough room for my shoulder blades across the cot, barely enough room for both of our bodies under the hunter's sag, but we managed somehow to complete the act and I discovered, for the first time in my life, that restraint can be very sexy.

Boone would usually fall right asleep and I'd be so tired from the day's hunting that I'd sleep too, even crushed like that under the weight of him. Sometime before three-thirty we'd wake up, stiff and numb, and he would slip out of my bunk and onto his knees on the floor. He'd stay there, kneeling for a while, rubbing my temples or massaging my fingers until I fell asleep again. When the alarm went off he was always buried in his sleeping bag, everything covered but one arm reaching toward my cot, sometimes still up and on the edge of it.

I don't think any of the hunters knew what was going on except for Russell, who got so crazy for Boone in his own way that he was afraid to leave Boone and me alone, afraid he'd miss a moment of intimacy, afraid even to fall asleep at night.

One night, close to climax, we bumped Russell hard, hard enough so that I felt it right through Boone. Boone lay still for a long time until we all fell asleep, and we never even finished making love. The next night we waited forever for Russell to start snoring, and even when he did I thought it sounded forced and fake but Boone seemed convinced by it and he crawled into my bed and made himself so flat like a snake against me that I couldn't tell my movements apart from his.

We hunted in grizzly-bear country, and on cloudy nights when the transistor could pick up the Fairbanks station we'd always hear of another mauling, or another hunter's body that Fish and Game couldn't find. We didn't go anywhere without rifles, and when our bush pilot found out I didn't have a gun he pulled the smallest .22 pistol I'd ever seen out of his pocket.

"It won't stop a bear unless you put it inside his mouth," he said. "But it's better than nothing at all."

And then he told a story just like all the other stories. In this one a bear took a man's scalp off with one swipe of the paw, and then the bear crushed his skull against a tree trunk, and then he broke his back against a rock.

But it wasn't the fear for my life that I thought would get to me, it wasn't the fighting or the hard work or the bad food. The only thing I really worried about in Alaska was how I'd feel when the hunt was successful, how I'd feel watching the animal go down: the period of time, however short, between the shooting and the dying.

Boone told me it wouldn't be as bad as I expected. He told me our hunters were expert marksmen, that they would all make perfect heart-lung shots, that the rams would die instantly and without pain. He told me that the good thing about hunting Dalls was that you always harvested the oldest rams because they were the ones with the biggest horns, they were the ones whose horns made a full curl. Boone said that most of the rams we would shoot that season would have died slow painful deaths of starvation that winter. He said when they got weak they would have had their guts ripped out by a pack of wolves, sometimes while they were still alive.

Boone talked a lot about the ethics of hunting, about the relationship between meat eaters and game. He said that even though he catered to trophy hunters he had never let his hunters shoot an animal without killing it, and had never let them kill one without taking all the meat. The scraps that had to be left on the carcass became food for the wolves and the eagles. It was the most basic of spiritual relationships, he said, and I wanted so much to believe him that I clung to his doctrine like hope.

But I still always rooted for the sheep. Whenever we got close I tried to send them telepathic messages to make them turn their heads and look at us, to make them run away after they'd seen us, but so often they would just stand there stupidly and wait to be shot. Sometimes they wouldn't move even after the hunter had fired, sometimes even after the dead ram had fallen at their feet.

It was at those times, in the middle of all the hand clasping, the stiff hugs and manly pats on the back, that I wondered how I could possibly be in love with Boone. I would wonder how I could possibly be in love with a man who seemed happy that the stunning white animal in front of us had just fallen dead.

The first sheep that died that season was for a hunter named James. James owned a company that manufactured all the essential components of sewage-treatment plants. He was jolly and a little stupid and evidently very rich.

On the first day we were all together, James told us a story about going hunting with six other men who all had elk permits. Apparently they all split up and James came upon the herd first and shot six animals in a matter of seconds. I tried to imagine coming into a clearing and seeing six bull elk and shooting all of them, not leaving even one.

"I knew if I just shot one they was gonna scatter and we'd lose them," he said. "They was standing real close together and I knew if I just let the lead fly, I'd dust more than one."

For the first ten days of James's hunt we had so much rain and such low clouds that the sheep could have been on top of us and we wouldn't have seen them. Our clothes had been wet for so long that our skin had started to rot underneath them. Each morning we put our feet into new plastic bags.

On the eleventh morning the sun came out bold and warm. During the cloudy days the short Alaskan summer had slipped into fall, and the tundra had already started to turn from green and yellow to orange and red.

Boone said our luck would change with the weather, and it wasn't two hours and six or seven miles of hiking before we'd spotted five of the biggest rams Boone had ever seen in the valley.

They were a long way from us, maybe three miles horizontal and three thousand feet up, the wind was squirrelly, and there was no real cover between us and them. Our only choice was to go right up the creek bed on our bellies and hope we blended with the moving water and the slate-colored rocks. The bed was steep for a couple of hundred yards, and there were two or three waterfalls to negotiate, and I thought we were going to lose James to the river once or twice, but we all made it through the steep part only half soaked.

Then we were in the tundra with almost no protection, and we had to crawl with our elbows and our boot tips, knees and stomachs in the mud, two or three inches per advance, wet, cold, dirty.

I thought how very much like soldiers we looked, how very much like war this all was, how very strange that the warlike element seemed to be so much the attraction.

The crawling took most of the day, and it put us in a good position for the afternoon feeding. We got behind a long low rock outcrop where we could get a good look at the rams, and sure enough, they had started coming down off the crags they bedded on during the day. Four of the five were full curls, all with a lot of mass and depth. We couldn't get any closer without being seen, so all we could do was lie on the rocks in our wet clothes and wait for them to graze in our direction.

Every half hour Boone would raise his body just enough to see over the ridge that protected us. He'd smile or give us the thumbs-up. Three more hours passed and the numbness which had started in my feet had worked its way up above my knees. Finally, Boone motioned for James to join him on the ridge. For the first time in hours I moved, getting up on my elbows to see the rams grazing, no more than a hundred yards away. I watched James try to position himself, try to breathe deeply, try to get the best hold on the gun. Boone was talking softly into his ear and I could only hear fragments of what he was saying—"very makeable shot," or "second from the right," "one chance," "get comfortable"—and I tried to imagine some rhythmic chant, some incantation, that would sanctify the scene somehow, that would make what seemed murderous holy. Then the shot exploded in my ears and one of the rams ran back up the mountain toward the crags.

"Watch him for blood!" Boone said to me. And I set my binoculars on him but he was climbing strong and steady. I was pretty sure it was a clean miss but I didn't say so because I didn't want James to get another shot, and the other four rams were still standing, staring, trying to get our scent, trying to understand what we were and what we were doing on their side of the mountain.

James was in position to shoot again.

"What do you see?" Boone asked me.

"I haven't got a look at him from the front," I said, which was true, even if beside the point.

James relaxed his hold on the gun. A gust of wind came suddenly from behind us and the rams got our scent. Just that fast they were climbing toward the fifth ram, and in seconds they were out of shooting range.

"He's clean," I said. "You must have shot over his back."

"Okay," Boone said to James. "We're gonna let them get a little ahead and then we're gonna follow them up to the top. Baby, I want you to stay here and watch the bottom. Watch the rams, watch our progress. Once we get to the top we're going to start to move south along the ridge. I want you to stay a few hundred yards ahead of us. I want you to keep the rams from coming down."

It was another three thousand feet to the top of the ridge. The rams topped out in twenty-five minutes. Boone and James hadn't gone a quarter of the way. I knew that if the rams would just keep going, if they would drop down into the debris on the other side, Boone and James would never get to them before dark.

I watched two rams butt horns against the darkening sky and I thought that maybe the reason why the ewes and the lambs lived separately was that the rams were not so different from the hunters after all, and in some strange way I was consoled.

"Go on," I thought at them again and again, but they stayed there, posed on the skyline while the men got closer.

Finally Boone and James were at the top, about six hundred yards from the rams. But the rams saw them first and started back down on my side. If I wanted to do as Boone told me, it was time to start walking. I sat in the tundra and slowly pulled on my gloves. I knew Boone could see me from up there. I knew he would know if I didn't do my job. I took a step toward where the rams were coming down, and then another. I had their attention, and they stalled nervously on the mountainside between the hunters and me. I sat down to change my socks, which were soaked and suddenly annoying. When I stood back up I watched the five rams, one at a time, slip down into the valley floor in front of me.

It was after dark when Boone and James got down off the mountain. We decided to camp there and look for the rams again early in the morning. I made some freeze-dried chicken stew and instant chocolate pudding.

Right after dinner we met Brian. He approached our camp at dusk, hollering for all he was worth so we wouldn't think he was a bear and fire. He walked and talked and looked like a Canadian lumberjack, but sometime during the evening he confessed to being from Philadelphia.

Brian was a survival specialist. He taught survival courses in Anchorage and nationwide. When he finished his two-week solo hunt he was off to the Sonoran desert to teach people how to jump out of helicopters with scuba gear on. He was the only man I met in Alaska who said nice things about his wife.

Brian carried Jack Daniel's in a plastic bottle that said "emergency provisions" in six different languages. He told us about his students; how they were required to solo for three days at the end of his course; how he gave them each a live rabbit to take with them so they could have one good meal. He hoped they would dry some jerky. He hoped they would stitch a hand warmer together with string made from the sinews in the rabbit's legs.

"But it never works," he said, "because companionship is a very special thing."

We all thought he was going to say something dirty, and we waited while he took a long hit off the bottle.

"I check on them sometime during the second day," he said. "They've all built little stone houses for their rabbits, some of them with mailboxes. They've given their rabbits names, and carved their initials into pieces of bark and hung them above the little doors."

We all sat there for a minute without saying anything, and then the conversation turned back to the usual. A brown bear that continued to charge after six rounds with a .300 Winchester. A bull moose that wouldn't go down after seven shots, and then after eight. A bullet that entered a caribou through the anus and exited through the mouth.

I looked across the fire in time to see Boone, out of chewing tobacco, stick a wad of instant coffee between his cheek and gum. Brian passed the bottle again, his rifle across his knees, a bullet in the chamber. He said he had followed grizzly prints the last mile and a half to camp, big ones, indicating at least a seven-foot bear.

I wanted to go to bed, but the tent was almost one hundred yards from the fire, and I knew I'd never get Boone away. I was tired of hunting stories, tired of chewing tobacco and cigars and the voices of men. I was tired of bear paranoia: of being afraid to spill one drop of food on my clothing, afraid to go to the bathroom, afraid to really fall asleep. I was tired of being cold and wet and hungry and thirsty and dirty and sweaty and clammy and tired of the sand that was in our eyes and our mouth and our food and our tent and even the water we drank and of the wind which blew it around and was incessant.

We never saw those five big rams again, but on the second-to-last day of James's hunt we got close enough to some new rams for another stalk. We had the wind in our favor but only a few hours till dark. We crawled like soldiers for what seemed like a long time, the only sound besides the river James's rhythmic grunting every time he lifted his belly out of the mud.

We got into shooting position with just enough light, Boone talking softly into James's ear, James positioning his body, then his rifle, then his body again. There were eleven rams in front of us, eight high and five low. At least four or five of them were full curls. I was trying to decide which one was the biggest when the gun fired sharp and loud, and then fired again.

"Don't shoot again!" Boone said, his voice angry. "Watch that ram."

And we all watched as one of the five lower rams ran down the gravel bed, his front legs splayed and awkward.

"Let me shoot again," James said. "Let me shoot at another one."

"We need to see if the one you shot at is hit," Boone said, calm again.

"He ain't hit," James said.

"He *is* hit," I said.

"At this point I can't tell," Boone said.

James cocked his gun.

The ram hobbled farther down and out of our view. James and Boone kept talking, talking themselves into the fact that the ram wasn't injured, but I knew it was. I knew it the way a mother knows when her child's been hurt.

"That ram's been hit," I said again. "I just don't know where."

First one and then three other rams ran down to join the first.

"I didn't see any blood," Boone said. "I think he's okay."

"He's not okay," I said, loudly now. "Do you hear me?"

Both men turned suddenly, as if remembering my presence for the first time, and then just as suddenly turned away.

"Let's see if we can get closer," Boone said. And then, after all that crawling, Boone stood up and strode across the moraine towards where the five lower rams had disappeared. James and I followed. The eight rams above us watched for a minute and then started climbing, slowly but steadily, up to the top of the ridge. The sun had set behind that ridge hours ago, but the Alaskan twilight lingered and lit the backdrop as the rams, one by one, topped out and filled the skyline, each one a perfect black silhouette against a bloody sky.

One of the five lower rams ran up to join the herd on the skyline. We came over a ledge and saw three more, not fifty feet below us.

"This is my kind of shot," James said.

"Not yet," Boone said. The three rams walked out in full view. None of them was bleeding.

"The first two are full curls," Boone said. "Fire when you're ready."

"We're still missing one ram," I said. "The injured ram is still down there."

Boone didn't even turn around. His hand silenced me. The gun fired again and the first ram went down.

"Dead ram!" Boone said.

I remember thinking I shouldn't watch, and I suspect everything would have been easier from then on if I hadn't. But it wasn't the way Boone had said it was going to be.

The ram was hit in the hindquarter, leaving him very much alive but unable to stand. For ten or twelve seconds he tried to drag himself across the glacier on his front feet, and then, exhausted, he gave up and started rolling down the glacier, rolling, in fact, right for a crevasse.

"Stop, you son of a bitch!" James yelled. "Stop, you motherfucker!"

The ram was still alive, twitching and kicking its front legs, when it fell several hundred feet to the bottom of the crevasse, irretrievable, even for the wolves, even for the eagles. We all watched the place where it had fallen.

"Jesus fuckin' Christ," James said.

That's when the injured ram, the first injured ram, limped out from the place we couldn't see below us and started to run, or tried to run, across the glacier. It was faltering now, dying, and we could see the blood running down between its front legs. Without a word to either of us, Boone grabbed James's gun and took off at a dead run across the glacier. Even fatally injured, the ram made better time on the ice than Boone, but just before the ram topped out above him he aimed and made a perfect heart-lung shot and the ram fell, instantly dead.

Of course we'd left our backpacks miles behind. Boone sent me back for them alone, and I clutched the little gun in my pocket as if it would help me. I walked right to the backpacks, in the near total darkness, something that even Boone himself couldn't have done. I had learned, by then, to make mental markers each time we left the packs, to find a mark on every surrounding horizon so that even after dark the spot could be relocated.

The temperature had dropped thirty degrees in thirty minutes, and I dug for my down coat and put it on over my wet clothing, and headed back toward James and Boone.

I found them just by following the smell of the dead ram. We were all without flashlights, and Boone decided it was too dark to butcher.

"We'll gut it and come back for it tomorrow," Boone said. "If the bears don't get it, the meat won't spoil."

"Fuck the meat," James said. "Let's cut the horns off the son of a bitch and get the hell out of here."

It was true dark now and James was getting nervous about bears. He had the safety off his gun and he kept spinning around every time a chunk of ice rolled down off the glacier.

"That's against the law," Boone said. "Come help me gut this ram." He turned to me. "You stay close."

I found out later about Alaska's wanton waste law, designed to protect the wilderness from trophy hunters like James. I also found out later the reason the ram smelled so awful. He died so slowly his adrenaline had lots of time to get pumping; James's first shot hit him in the gut and by the time he finally died his insides were rotten with stomach acid.

That night, though, the smell just seemed like a natural part of the nightmare. Even when they were finished gutting and we all started gingerly down the glacier, the smell of the ram came off Boone like he was the one who'd been shot in the gut. For the first time ever, I wouldn't hug him. He saved me from slipping once by grabbing my hand and left the smell all over my glove. It was worse than sour milk, that smell, worse than cat piss, worse than anything.

We walked for over an hour and I could tell by my marks on the skyline that we hadn't even gone a half a mile.

"This is crazy," I said. It was so dark that we couldn't see the dirty ice we walked on. "One of us is going to wind up in a crevasse with that ram."

"Maybe we should sit for a couple hours," Boone said. "If we sit for three or four hours it will start getting light."

"I think we should keep walking," James said.

Neither option was good. We were wet and cold already, we smelled like dinner for a bear, we had one real gun and a hunter who couldn't make an accurate shot at thirty yards. But we were alive and whole and together, and each careful step I took into the blackness made my heart race.

"We'll sit until we get so cold we have to move again," Boone said.

We piled up, nearly on top of each other. I opened three cans of sardines.

"That's perfect," Boone said. "The bear will think he's getting surf and turf."

We did okay for the first half hour. There had been a light cloud cover at sunset but now a million stars dotted the moonless sky. Boone was the thinnest, and he started to shiver first. We moved even closer together.

My fantasies were simple. A long hot shower. A plate of vegetables. A bed with sheets. TV. I thought of my mother, our last conversation by satellite telephone from North Pole, Alaska, where I assured her there was no real danger, and she told me about an actor, Jimmy Stewart or Paul Newman. "He used to be an avid hunter," she said, "and now he's a conser-

vationist. He's done a hundred-and-eighty-degree switch."
And I stood there for five dollars a minute listening to myself
tell her that conservation and hunting are not antithetical,
listening to myself use words like "game management,"
words like "harvest" and "herd control."

"This," I said out loud, "is wanting to love somebody too
much."

"Here come the lights," Boone said, and even as he said
the words a translucent green curtain began to rise on the
horizon. Then the curtain divided itself and became a wave
and the wave divided itself and became a dragon, then a
goddess, then a wave. Soon the whole night sky was full of
spirits flying and rolling, weaving and braiding themselves
across the sky. The colors were familiar, mostly shades of
green, but the motion, the movement, was unearthly and
somehow female; it was unlike anything I'd ever seen. I was
suddenly warm with amazement. I pressed my body harder
into Boone's.

Early the next morning we went back for the ram. I shot a
roll of film while James and Boone hugged and shook hands
over it, while they picked up the horns and twisted the now
stiff head from side to side, and then shook hands again. They
were happy as schoolboys and I understood that what we had
accomplished was more for this moment than anything, this
moment where two men were allowed to be happy together
and touch.

James flew back to Fairbanks the next morning, giving
Boone and me our first day together in more than two weeks.
We needed to take another hundred pounds of food up to the
cabin for the hunter who was already on his way, and bring
the garbage back down to the strip. With the six miles of

packing each way from the airstrip we had a full day, but I was hoping we'd have time for a nice lunch once we got up there, hoping we'd have time for some loud, rowdy sex before we had to load up our packs and come back down.

The sun came out for our walk to the cabin, and when we got there I made Boone lunch and a couple of drinks. I mixed the Tang and water separately from the rum so the drinks would taste real. I added extra butter to the freeze-dried food, some dehydrated Parmesan, some parsley flakes.

I can't remember how the fight started, or why we disagreed. I only remember the moment when we stepped, as we always did, out of ourselves, and into the roles from which we fight.

"I spent the whole day trying to make everything nice for you," I said, hearing the script in my head, already knowing the outcome of the scene.

"What did you do?" he said. "Boil water?"

And he was right, what I had done was boil water, and there still might have been a way of saving the day if it hadn't been for the fact of those parsley flakes, if it hadn't been for the fact of that Parmesan cheese.

"Go to hell," I said.

"What was that?"

"Fuck you."

And then he was there, in my face, temples bulging. He grabbed my neck and twisted it into an unnatural position. I felt one of the lenses fall out of my glasses, felt something pinch between my shoulder blades, and I screamed, trying to channel all the pain into my voice so he'd let go, and it worked. But then he came back at me, grabbed my shirt around my neck and twisted it.

"If you hurt me again," I said, "I'll shoot you." It was sort of a ridiculous thing to say, on many levels, not the least of which being that the gun in my pocket, the one that Bill had given me simply out of pity, wasn't big enough to kill a ptarmigan unless you hit it in exactly the right place. I remembered another argument of months before, where I'd said I wouldn't shoot a rapist and infuriated Boone, and I tried to decide if what was happening was somehow worse than rape, and I knew even then that Boone would never really hurt me and I would never really shoot him, loving him like I did. And I decided it was just something I said because it seemed like the next logical line in the drama, but it made Boone wilder.

He ripped my coat off and took the little gun out of my pocket. He knocked me onto the floor of the cabin and then picked me up and threw me out the front door. My knee hit the rock that was the doorstop. He threw my backpack out after me, and then my bag of dirty clothes. The wind coming off the glacier picked up one of my T-shirts, a couple of pairs of underwear, and scattered them across the tundra, which was finally, I noticed, all red and gold.

"Give me my gun," I said, as if that were the issue.

"You won't have it," he said. "And don't ask again."

Stupid in his anger, he walked to the river, leaving his rifle a few feet away from me. I stared at it for a minute and thought about my previously nonviolent life. Only rednecks and crazy people had fights with guns, people in the inner city, people on late-night news shows.

But I was fascinated by us with our dramatics, and somehow bound to the logical sequence of the scene. I picked up the rifle, carried it into the cabin, hid it under a foam pad on the bunk bed, and sat on it.

"Where is it?" he said, minutes later. "Did you touch it?" I knew in his anger he thought he might have misplaced his gun. He crashed around the cabin and then outside.

"Where is it?" he said again.

"Give me my gun," I said.

This undid him. He ripped his gun out from under me.

"If you messed up the scope . . ." he said. I eased into the corner as he examined the scope. If it had moved a fraction, even if only in his mind, I was in big trouble. We had gone too far this time, and at that instant I didn't know if and how we'd ever get back. He put his rifle down and took a step toward me.

"Don't come near me," I said.

"Now don't get upset," he said, suddenly all control and condescension. "Just get yourself together." He patted my knee. "Take it easy now," he said. "Take a deep breath."

That was when my hiking boot moved, it seemed, all by itself and my Vibram sole connected with his thigh and I pushed with all the strength I had and sent him hurtling backwards across the cabin into the woodpile and the stove. A shelf crashed down on his head when he hit the wall. My foot hung in the air and I stared at it, amazed at its power, amazed at my life's first violent act.

Then Boone was up and coming across the cabin at me and I just balled up and let him throw me out the door again, let my knee make contact with the rock. I gathered my clothes around me, pulled my backpack over my legs to block the wind.

Boone stayed inside, shouting things I only half heard. "You're out," he said at one point. "In more ways than you know."

I thought I ought to be horrified at myself, but I felt okay, light-headed, almost elated. He was stronger but I was strong. I looked again at my boot and flexed the muscle in my leg.

His tirade ended in some kind of a question I couldn't hear but guessed was rhetorical. I said something I couldn't resist about the shoe being on the other foot, and then laughed out loud so suddenly that he came to the cabin door and stared at me.

It was going to be dark in a few hours and I didn't think Boone would let me in the cabin, so I gathered up my under-wear and started down towards the airstrip, where we had a tent set up. I knew it was a bad time of night to be walking alone in bear country, but after two long weeks without even seeing one bear, the grizzly had started to seem a bit like a creature of everybody's mind.

My knee was swelling to almost twice its normal size, but as long as I watched where I was walking, and didn't let it bend too far, it didn't really hurt. It was because I was looking down, I guess, because I was walking carefully, that I got so close to the bears before we saw each other.

It was a sow, six or seven feet tall, and two nearly full-grown cubs. They were knee-deep in blueberries, rolling and eating and playing. When I saw them they weren't fifty yards away.

I froze, and reached for my little gun before I remembered that Boone hadn't given it back. I took one step backwards and that's when mama saw me. The sun was just setting, and the late-afternoon light shone off their coats, which were brown and long and frosted at the tips. Mama stood on her hind legs, all seven feet of her, and then the cubs stood too and looked my way. They couldn't smell me, I knew, and they were trying to. Mama's ears went back and I thought, "Here she comes," but then she raised one giant paw in the air and swung it at me like a forehand, and then all three bears ran up into the mountain.

Boone and I took three more hunters out that season and we got them each a ram. All three hunters made perfect heart-lung shots. All three rams died instantly, just like Boone said.

One of our hunters, a man named Chuck, was kind and sincere. He got his ram with a bow and arrow from thirty yards away after a ten-hour stalk that was truly artistic. Chuck seemed to have an unspoken understanding with the wild-lands and I was really almost happy for him when the ram went down, and I would have shaken his hand when he and Boone got finished jumping up and down in each other's arms if he had wanted to shake mine.

Boone told me I would get used to watching the rams die, and I have to admit—not without a certain horror—that the third killing was easier than the second, and the fourth was easier yet again.

I got thinner and harder and stronger and faster, turning my body into the kind of machine I couldn't help but be proud of, even though that had never been my goal.

Boone and I stopped fighting after the day we hiked to the cabin, but we also stopped talking; what we had left between us was hunting, and making love. I knew as soon as we got back to the lower forty-eight it would be over between us, and so I spent each day hiking behind him, measuring the time by quantity and not quality. It was like sitting by the bedside of a dying friend.

The nights got longer and longer, and we spent a lot more of them stuck out and away from the cabin. But the clouds were always thick and low, and even on the nights I tried hard to stay awake the northern lights never came again.

It was late September when we finished. The snow line was below four thousand feet and it was getting well below zero every night, and we'd been camped on the airstrip for three days waiting for the bush plane. The last hunters had flown out days before, and Boone and I had closed up the cabin in silence, like animals preparing for winter.

It had been hours, maybe days, since we'd spoken, so the sound of Boone's voice out of the darkness, out of somewhere deep in his sleeping bag, startled me.

"You know, none of those rams had an ounce of fat on them," he said. "There's not one of them that would have lasted through the winter."

"Well," I said. "That's something."

"I've been doing this for years," he said, and at first I thought he was going to say, "And it still isn't easy to watch them die," but he didn't.

"You really hung in there," he said.

"Yeah," I said. "I did."

"But it made you stop loving me," he said. "Even so."

Somewhere up the mountain the wolves started moaning and shrieking. I hadn't told Boone about the night I saw the bears, but the scene had stayed right with me; I couldn't get it out of my mind. It was the power of the mother bear's gesture, I guess, the power and the ambivalence. Because the wave of her paw was both forbidding and inviting. Because even though I knew that she was showing me her anger, I also knew that somewhere in her gesture, she was asking me to come along.

Cowboys Are My Weakness

I have a picture in my mind of a tiny ranch on the edge of a stand of pine trees with some horses in the yard. There's a woman standing in the doorway in cutoffs and a blue chambray work shirt and she's just kissed her tall, bearded, and soft-spoken husband goodbye. There's laundry hanging outside and the morning sun is filtering through the tree branches like spiderwebs. It's the morning after a full moon, and behind the house the deer have eaten everything that was left in the garden.

If I were a painter, I'd paint that picture just to see if the girl in the doorway would turn out to be me. I've been out west ten years now, long enough to call it my home, long enough to know I'll be here forever, but I still don't know where that ranch is. And even though I've had plenty of men here, some of them tall and nearly all of them bearded, I still haven't met the man who has just walked out of the painting, who has just started his pickup truck, whose tire marks I can still see in the sandy soil of the drive.

The west isn't a place that gives itself up easily. Newcomers have to sink into it slowly, to descend through its layers, and I'm still descending. Like most easterners, I started out in the transitional zones, the big cities and the ski towns that outsiders have set up for their own comfort, the places so often referred to as "the best of both worlds." But I was bound to work my way back, through the land, into the small towns and beyond them. That's half the reason I wound up on a ranch near Grass Range, Montana; the other half is Homer.

I've always had this thing about cowboys, maybe because I was born in New Jersey. But a real cowboy is hard to find these days, even in the west. I thought I'd found one on several occasions, I even at one time thought Homer was a cowboy, and though I loved him like crazy for a while and in some ways always will, somewhere along the line I had to face the fact that even though Homer looked like a cowboy, he was just a capitalist with a Texas accent who owned a horse.

Homer's a wildlife specialist in charge of a whitetail deer management project on the ranch. He goes there every year to observe the deer from the start of the mating season in late October until its peak in mid-November. It's the time when the deer are most visible, when the bucks get so lusty they lose their normal caution, when the does run around in the middle of the day with their white tails in the air. When Homer talked me into coming with him, he said I'd love the ranch, and I did. It was sixty miles from the nearest paved road. All of the buildings were whitewashed and plain. One of them had been ordered from a 1916 Sears catalogue. The ranch hands still rode horses, and when the late-afternoon light swept the grainfields across from headquarters, I would watch them move the cattle in rows that looked like waves. There was a peace about the ranch that was uncanny and might have been complete if not for the eight or nine hungry barn cats that crawled up your legs if you even smelled like food, and the exotic chickens of almost every color that fought all day in their pens.

Homer has gone to the ranch every year for the last six, and he has a long history of stirring up trouble there. The ranch hands watch him sit on the hillside and hate him for the money he makes. He's slept with more than one or two of their wives and girlfriends. There was even some talk that he was the reason the ranch owner got divorced.

When he asked me to come with him I knew it would be me or somebody else and I'd heard good things about Montana so I went. There was a time when I was sure Homer was the man who belonged in my painting and I would have sold my soul to be his wife, or even his only girlfriend. I'd come close, in the spring, to losing my mind because of it, but I had finally learned that Homer would always be separate, even from himself, and by the time we got to Montana I was almost immune to him.

Homer and I live in Fort Collins, Colorado, most of the year, in houses that are exactly one mile apart. He's out of town as often as not, keeping track of fifteen whitetail deer herds all across the West. I go with him when he lets me, which is lately more and more. The herds Homer studies are isolated by geography, given plenty of food in bad winters, and protected from hunters and wolves. Homer is working on reproduction and genetics, trying to create, in the wild, super-bucks bigger and tougher than elk. The Montana herd has been his most successful, so he spends the long mating season there. Under his care the bucks have shown incredible increases in antler mass, in body weight, and in fertility.

The other scientists at the university that sponsors Homer respect him, not only for his success with the deer, but for his commitment to observation, for his relentless dedication to his hours in the field. They also think he is eccentric and a bit overzealous.

At first I thought he just liked to be outdoors, but when we got to the ranch his obsession with the deer made him even more like a stranger. He was gone every day from way before sunrise till long after dark. He would dress all in camouflage, even his gloves and socks, and sit on the hillsides above where the deer fed and watch, making notes a few times an hour, changing position every hour or two. If I went with him I wasn't allowed to move except when he did, and I was never allowed to talk. I'd try to save things up for later that I thought of during the day, but by the time we got back to our cabin they seemed unimportant and Homer liked to eat his dinner in front of the TV. By the time we got the dishes done it was way past Homer's bedtime. We were making love less and less, and when we did, it was always from behind.

The ranch owner's name was David, and he wasn't what you'd think a Montana ranch owner would be. He was a poet, and a vegetarian. He listened to Andreas Vollenweider and drank hot beverages with names like Suma and Morning Rain. He wouldn't let the ranch hands use pesticides or chemicals, he wouldn't hire them if they smoked cigarettes. He undergrazed the ranch by about fifty percent, so the organic grain was belly-high to a horse almost everywhere.

David had an idea about recreating on his forty thousand acres the Great Plains that only the Indians and the first settlers had seen. He wasn't making a lot of money ranching, but he was producing the fattest, healthiest, most organic Black Angus cattle in North America. He was sensitive, thoughtful, and kind. He was the kind of man I always knew I should fall in love with, but never did.

Homer and David ate exactly one dinner a week together, which I always volunteered to cook. Homer was always polite and full of incidental conversation and much too quick to laugh. David was quiet and sullen and so restrained that he was hard to recognize.

The irreconcilable differences between Homer and me had been revealing themselves one at a time since late summer. In early November I asked him what he wanted to do on Thanksgiving, and he said he'd like most of all to stay on the ranch and watch the does in heat.

Homer was only contracted to work on the ranch until the Sunday before Thanksgiving. When he asked me to come with him he told me we would leave the ranch in plenty of time to have the holidays at home.

I was the only child in a family that never did a lot of celebrating because my parents couldn't plan ahead. They were sun worshipers, and we spent every Thanksgiving in a plane on the way to Puerto Rico, every Christmas in a car on Highway 95, heading for Florida. What I remember most from those days is Casey Kasem's Christmas shows, the long-distance dedications, "I'll be home for Christmas" from Bobby D. in Spokane to Linda S. in Decatur. We never had hotel reservations and the places we wound up in had no phones and plastic mattress covers and triple locks on the doors. Once we spent Christmas night parked under a fluorescent streetlight, sleeping in the car.

I've spent most of the holidays in my adult life making up

for those road trips. I spend lots of money on hand-painted ornaments. I always cook a roast ten pounds bigger than anything we could possibly eat.

Homer thinks my enthusiasm about holidays is childish and self-serving. To prove it to me, last Christmas morning he set the alarm for six-thirty and went back to his house to stain a door. This year I wanted Thanksgiving in my own house. I wanted to cook a turkey we'd be eating for weeks.

I said, "Homer, you've been watching the deer for five weeks now. What else do you think they're gonna do?"

"You don't know anything about it," he said. "Thanksgiving is the premium time. Thanksgiving," he shook one finger in the air, "is the height of the rut."

David and I drank tea together, and every day took walks up into the canyon behind ranch headquarters. He talked about his ex-wife, Carmen, about the red flowers that covered the canyon walls in June, about imaging away nuclear weapons. He told me about the woman Homer was sleeping with on the ranch the year before, when I was back in Colorado counting days till he got home. She was the woman who took care of the chickens, and David said that when Homer left the ranch she wrote a hundred love songs and made David listen while she sang them all.

"She sent them on a tape to Homer," David said, "and when he didn't call or write, she went a little nuts. I finally told her to leave the ranch. I'm not a doctor, and we're a long way from anywhere out here."

From the top of the canyon we could see Homer's form blending with the trees on the ridge above the garden, where the deer ate organic potatoes by the hundreds of pounds.

"I understand if he wasn't interested anymore," David

said. "But I can't believe even he could ignore a gesture that huge."

We watched Homer crawl along the ridge from tree to tree. I could barely distinguish his movements from what the wind did to the tall grass. None of the deer below him even turned their heads.

"What is it about him?" David said, and I knew he was looking for an explanation about Carmen, but I'd never even met her and I didn't want to talk about myself.

"Homer's always wearing camouflage," I said. "Even when he's not."

The wind went suddenly still and we could hear, from headquarters, the sounds of cats fighting, a hen's frantic scream, and then, again, the cats.

David put his arm around me. "We're such good people," he said. "Why aren't we happy?"

One day when I got back from my walk with David, Homer was in the cabin in the middle of the day. He had on normal clothes and I could tell he'd shaved and showered. He took me into the bedroom and climbed on top of me frontwards, the way he did when we first met and I didn't even know what he did for a living.

Afterwards he said, "We didn't need a condom, did we?" I counted the days forward and backward and forward again. Homer always kept track of birth control and groceries and gas mileage and all the other things I couldn't keep my mind on. Still, it appeared to be exactly ten days before my next period.

"Yes," I said. "I think we did."

Homer has never done an uncalculated thing in his life,

and for a moment I let myself entertain the possibility that his mistake meant that somewhere inside he wanted to have a baby with me, that he really wanted a family and love and security and the things I thought everybody wanted before I met Homer. On the other hand, I knew that one of the ways I had gotten in trouble with Homer, and with other men before him, was by inventing thoughts for them that they'd never had.

"Well," he said. "In that case we better get back to Colorado before they change the abortion laws."

Sometimes the most significant moments of your life reveal themselves to you even as they are happening, and I knew in that moment that I would never love Homer the same way again. It wasn't so much that not six months before, when I had asked Homer what we'd do if I got pregnant, he said we'd get married and have a family. It wasn't even that I was sure I wanted a baby. It wasn't even that I thought there was going to be a baby to want.

It all went back to the girl in the log cabin, and how the soft-spoken man would react if she thought she was going to have a baby. It would be winter now, and snowing outside the windows warm with yellow light. He might dance with the sheepdog on the living-room floor, he might sing the theme song from *Father Knows Best,* he might go out and do a swan dive into the snow.

I've been to a lot of school and read a lot of thick books, but at my very core there's a made-for-TV-movie mentality I don't think I'll ever shake. And although there's a lot of doubt in my mind about whether or not an ending as simple and happy as I want is possible anymore in the world, it was clear to me that afternoon that it wasn't possible with Homer.

Five o'clock the next morning was the first time I saw the real cowboy. He was sitting in the cookhouse eating cereal and I couldn't make myself sleep next to Homer so I'd been up all night wandering around.

He was tall and thin and bearded. His hat was white and ratty and you could tell by looking at his stampede strap that it had been made around a campfire after lots of Jack Daniel's. I'd had my fingers in my hair for twelve hours and my face was breaking out from too much stress and too little sleep and I felt like such a greaseball that I didn't say hello. I poured myself some orange juice, drank it, rinsed the glass, and put it in the dish drainer. I took one more look at the cowboy, and walked back out the door, and went to find Homer in the field.

Homer's truck was parked by a culvert on the South Fork road, which meant he was walking the brush line below the cliffs that used to be the Blackfeet buffalo jumps. It was a boneyard down there, the place where hundreds of buffalo, chased by the Indians, had jumped five hundred feet to their death, and the soil was extremely fertile. The grass was thicker and sweeter there than anywhere on the ranch, and Homer said the deer sucked calcium out of the buffalo bones. I saw Homer crouched at the edge of a meadow I couldn't get to without being seen, so I went back and fell asleep in the bed of his truck.

It was hunting season, and later that morning Homer and I found a deer by the side of the road that had been poached but not taken. The poacher must have seen headlights or heard a truck engine and gotten scared.

I lifted the back end of the animal into the truck while Homer picked up the antlers. It was a young buck, two and a half at the oldest, but it would have been a monster in a few years, and I knew Homer was taking the loss pretty hard.

We took it down to the performance center, where they weigh the organic calves. Homer attached a meat hook to its antlers and hauled it into the air above the pickup.

"Try and keep it from swinging," he said. And I did my best, considering I wasn't quite tall enough to get a good hold, and its blood was bubbling out of the bullet hole and dripping down on me.

That's when the tall cowboy, the one from that morning, walked out of the holding pen behind me, took a long slow look at me trying to steady the back end of the dead deer, and settled himself against the fence across the driveway. I stepped back from the deer and pushed the hair out of my eyes. He raised one finger to call me over. I walked slow and didn't look back at Homer.

"Nice buck," he said. "Did you shoot it?"

"It's a baby," I said. "I don't shoot animals. A poacher got it last night."

"Who was the poacher?" he said, and tipped his hat just past my shoulder toward Homer.

"You're wrong," I said. "You can say a lot of things about him, but he wouldn't poach a deer."

"My name's Montrose T. Coty," he said. "Everyone calls me Monte."

I shook his hand. "Everyone calls you Homer's girl-friend," he said, "but I bet that's not your name."

"You're right," I said, "it's not."

I turned to look at Homer. He was taking measurements off the hanging deer: antler length, body length, width at its girth.

"Tonight's the Stockgrowers' Ball in Grass Range," Monte said. "I thought you might want to go with me."

Homer was looking into the deer's hardened eyeballs. He had its mouth open, and was pulling on its tongue.

"I have to cook dinner for Homer and David," I said. "I'm sorry. It sounds like fun."

In the car on the way back to the cabin, Homer said, "What was that all about?"

I said, "Nothing," and then I said, "Monte asked me to the Stockgrowers' Ball."

"The Stockgrowers' Ball?" he said. "Sounds like a great time. What do stockgrowers do at a ball?" he said. "Do they dance?"

I almost laughed with him until I remembered how much I loved to dance. I'd been with Homer chasing whitetail so long that I'd forgotten that dancing, like holidays, was something I loved. And I started to wonder just then what else being with Homer had made me forget. Hadn't I, at one time, spent whole days listening to music? Wasn't there a time when I wanted, more than anything, to buy a sailboat? And didn't I love to be able to go outdoors and walk anywhere I wanted, and to make, if I wanted, all kinds of noise?

I wanted to blame Homer, but I realized then it was more my fault than his. Because even though I'd never let the woman in the chambray work shirt out of my mind I'd let her, in the last few years, become someone different, and she wasn't living, anymore, in my painting. The painting she was living in, I saw, belonged to somebody else.

"So what did you tell him?" Homer said.

"I told him I'd see if you'd cook dinner," I said.

I tried to talk to Homer before I left. First I told him that it wasn't a real date, that I didn't even know Monte, and really I was only going because I didn't know if I'd ever have another chance to go to a Stockgrowers' Ball. When he didn't answer at all I worked up to saying that maybe it was a good idea for me to start seeing other people. That maybe we'd had two different ideas all along and we needed to find two other people who would better meet our needs. I told him that if he had any opinions I wished he'd express them to me, and he thought for a few minutes and then he said,

"Well, I guess we have Jimmy Carter to thank for all the trouble in Panama."

I spent the rest of the day getting ready for the Stockgrowers' Ball. All I'd brought with me was some of Homer's camouflage and blue jeans, so I wound up borrowing a skirt that David's ex-wife had left behind, some of the chicken woman's dress shoes that looked ridiculous and made my feet huge, and a vest that David's grandfather had been shot at in by the Plains Indians.

Monte had to go into town early to pick up ranch supplies, so I rode in with his friends Buck and Dawn, who spent the whole drive telling me what a great guy Monte was, how he quit the rodeo circuit to make a decent living for himself and his wife, how she'd left without saying goodbye not six months before.

They told me that he'd made two thousand dollars in one afternoon doing a Wrangler commercial. That he'd been in a laundromat on his day off and the director had seen him through the window, had gone in and said, "Hey, cowboy, you got an hour? You want to make two thousand bucks?"

"Ole Monte," Buck said. "He's the real thing."

After an hour and a half of washboard road we pulled into the dance hall just on our edge of town. I had debated about wearing the cowboy hat I'd bought especially for my trip to Montana, and was thankful I'd decided against it. It was clear, once inside, that only the men wore hats, and only dress hats at that. The women wore high heels and stockings and in almost every case hair curled away from their faces in great airy rolls.

We found Monte at a table in the corner, and the first thing he did was give me a corsage, a pink one, mostly roses that couldn't have clashed more with my rust-colored blouse. Dawn pinned it on me, and I blushed, I suppose, over my first corsage in ten years, and a little old woman in spike heels leaned over and said, "Somebody loves you!" just loud enough for Monte and Buck and Dawn to hear.

During dinner they showed a movie about a cattle drive. After dinner a young enthusiastic couple danced and sang for over an hour about cattle and ranch life and the Big Sky, a phrase which since I'd been in Montana had seemed perpetually on the tip of everybody's tongue.

After dinner the dancing started, and Monte asked me if I knew how to do the Montana two-step. He was more than a foot taller than me, and his hat added another several inches to that. When we stood on the dance floor my eyes came right to the place where his silk scarf disappeared into the shirt buttons on his chest. His big hands were strangely light on me and my feet went the right direction even though my mind couldn't remember the two-step's simple form.

"That's it," he said into the part in my hair. "Don't think. Just let yourself move with me."

And we were moving together, in turns that got tighter and tighter each time we circled the dance floor. The songs got faster and so did our motion until there wasn't time for anything but the picking up and putting down of feet, for the swirling colors of Carmen's ugly skirt, for breath and sweat and rhythm.

I was farther west than I'd ever imagined, and in the strange, nearly flawless synchronization on the dance floor I knew I could be a Montana ranch woman, and I knew I could make Monte my man. It had taken me ten years, and an incredible sequence of accidents, but that night I thought I'd finally gotten where I'd set out to go.

The band played till two and we danced till three to the jukebox. Then there was nothing left to do but get in the car and begin the two-hour drive home.

First we talked about our horses. It was the logical choice, the only thing we really had in common, but it only lasted twenty minutes.

I tried to get his opinion on music and sailing, but just like a cowboy, he was too polite for me to tell anything for sure.

Then we talked about the hole in my vest that the Indians shot, which I was counting on, and half the reason I wore it.

The rest of the time we just looked at the stars.

I had spent a good portion of the night worrying about what I was going to say when Monte asked me to go to bed with him. When he pulled up between our two cabins he looked at me sideways and said,

"I'd love to give you a great big kiss, but I've got a mouthful of chew."

I could hear Homer snoring before I got past the kitchen.

Partly because I didn't like the way Monte and Homer eyed each other, but mostly because I couldn't bear to spend Thanksgiving watching does in heat, I loaded my gear in my truck and got ready to go back to Colorado.

On the morning I left, Homer told me that he had decided that I was the woman he wanted to spend the rest of his life with after all, and that he planned to go to town and buy a ring just as soon as the rut ended.

He was sweet on my last morning on the ranch, generous and attentive in a way I'd never seen. He packed me a sack lunch of chicken salad he mixed himself, and he went out to my car and dusted off the inch of snow that had fallen in our first brush with winter, overnight. He told me to call when I got to Fort Collins, he even said to call collect, but I suppose one of life's big tricks is to give us precisely the thing we want, two weeks after we've stopped wanting it, and I couldn't take Homer seriously, even when I tried.

When I went to say goodbye to David he hugged me hard, said I was welcome back on the ranch anytime. He said he enjoyed my company and appreciated my insight. Then he said he liked my perfume and I wondered where my taste in men had come from, I wondered whoever taught me to be so stupid about men.

I knew Monte was out riding the range, so I left a note on his car thanking him again for the dancing and saying I'd be back one day and we could dance again. I put my hat on, that Monte had never got to see, and rolled out of headquarters. It was the middle of the day, but I saw seven bucks in the first five miles, a couple of them giants, and when I slowed down they just stood and stared at the truck. It was the height of the rut and Homer said that's how they'd be, love-crazed and fearless as bears.

About a mile before the edge of ranch property, I saw something that looked like a lone antelope running across the skyline, but antelope are almost never alone, so I stopped the car to watch. As the figure came closer I saw it was a horse, a big chestnut, and it was carrying a rider at a full gallop, and it was coming right for the car.

I knew it could have been any one of fifty cowboys employed on the ranch, and yet I've learned to expect more from life than that, and so in my heart I knew it was Monte. I got out of the car and waited, pleased that he'd see my hat most of all, wondering what he'd say when I said I was leaving.

He didn't get off his horse, which was sweating and shaking so hard I thought it might die while we talked.

"You on your way?" he said.

I smiled and nodded. His chaps were sweat-soaked, his leather gloves worn white.

"Will you write me a letter?" he said.

"Sure," I said.

"Think you'll be back this way?" he asked.

"If I come back," I said, "will you take me dancing?"

"Damn right," he said, and a smile that seemed like the smile I'd been waiting for my whole life spread wide across his face.

"Then it'll be sooner than later," I said.

He winked and touched the horse's flank with his spurs and it hopped a little on the takeoff and then there was just dirt flying while the high grass swallowed the horse's legs. I leaned against the door of my pickup truck watching my new cowboy riding off toward where the sun was already low in the sky and the grass shimmering like nothing I'd ever seen in the mountains. And for a minute I thought we were living inside my painting, but he was riding away too fast to tell. And I wondered then why I had always imagined my cowboy's truck as it was leaving. I wondered why I hadn't turned the truck around and painted my cowboy coming home.

There's a story—that isn't true—that I tell about myself when I first meet someone, about riding a mechanical bull in a bar. In the story, I stay on through the first eight levels of difficulty, getting thrown on level nine only after dislocating my thumb and winning my boyfriend, who was betting on me, a big pile of money. It was something I said in a bar one night, and I liked the way it sounded so much I kept telling it. I've been telling it for so many years now, and in such scrupulous detail, that it has become a memory and it's hard for me to remember that it isn't true. I can smell the smoke and beer-soaked carpets, I can hear the cheers of all the men. I can see the bar lights blur and spin, and I can feel the cold iron buck between my thighs, the painted saddle slam against my tail-bone, the surprise and pain when my thumb extends too far and I let go. It's a good story, a story that holds my listeners' attention, and although I consider myself almost pathologically honest, I have somehow allowed myself this one small lie.

And watching Monte ride off through the long grains, I thought about the way we invent ourselves through our stories, and in a similar way, how the stories we tell put walls around our lives. And I think that may be true about cowboys. That there really isn't much truth in my saying cowboys are my weakness; maybe, after all this time, it's just something I've learned how to say.

I felt the hoofbeats in the ground long after Monte's white shirt and ratty hat melded with the sun. When I couldn't even pretend to feel them anymore, I got in the car and headed for the hard road.

I listened to country music the whole way to Cody, Wyoming. The men in the songs were all either brutal or inexpressive and always sorry later. The women were victims, every one. I started to think about coming back to the ranch to visit Monte, about another night dancing, about another night wanting the impossible love of a country song, and I thought:

This is not my happy ending.

This is not my story.

Jackson Is Only One of My Dogs

I have a dog named Jackson, who between the ages of four and five, in people years, became suicidal. In a period of less than twelve months, Jackson jumped out of the back of a speeding pickup truck, ate a fourteen-pound bag of nonorganic garden fertilizer, and threw himself between the jaws of a hundred-and-fifty-pound Russian wolfhound. Similarly, when I turned twenty-eight years old, I started to date a man whose favorite song was "Desperado."

He was an outdoorsman, in his heart, but for a living he rebuilt old homes with a passion that was uncanny, and never wasted on me. He had skin stretched so tight across his muscles I sometimes thought his legs would pop. He was smart and selfish and lied by omission. I was addicted to him like cough syrup, and I didn't respect his mind.

My friend Debra said, "He's not an altogether bad person. He just has no imagination, and of course, that has made him a little mean."

For two whole years I danced around my lover like a top, like wheat grass, like light. I stripped the linoleum off all his hardwood floors. I learned to snowshoe and fly-fish and box. He would finger the rose-colored trout that I caught, he would run his hand along the wood's fine grain, he would look through me at a window that needed painting, and through it to a meadow, a mountain, some sport he hadn't yet tried.

I told Debra about the passion, the hours in bed, the best (I actually said this) sex I had ever had, and as I said the words I believed them to be true. I didn't tell her about the time he got out of bed during foreplay and I found him, twenty minutes later, naked and caulking the bathtub. I didn't tell her that in all the times he's been inside me, he's never once met my eyes.

Jackson is only one of my dogs. The other dog, the good dog, whose name is Hailey, passed through her early adulthood without any discernible personality changes. Hailey is matronly and brindle-colored, with a rear end that is slightly out of alignment. Jackson is shaggy and blond, all ears and feathers.

While Jackson is clearly a human being trapped in a dog's body (one day he lost his senses and buried a bone in the yard and I was no more embarrassed for him than he was for himself), Hailey knows what she is and is proud of it. What she likes to do, more than anything, is to get her belly wet and then lie around in the dirt. Jackson is athletic, graceful, obnoxious, and filled with conceit, while Hailey is slow, a little fat, and gentle to her bones.

Jackson also has a truck neurosis. His whole life is centered around making sure that the truck I drive doesn't leave without him. When he is in the house he keeps one eye on it in the driveway, when we're on the road I never have to tell him to stay. It's where he likes to eat and drink, where he wants to spend his afternoons; it's the only place he'll let himself sleep soundly. Sometimes, when we are backpacking, and thirty miles from anywhere, I'll say, "Go get in the truck, Jackson," just to play with his mind.

By the time I turned twenty-eight years old I had broken five major bones in my body. The only appendage that is still straight is my right arm.

People say, "Are your bones particularly brittle?" They say, "Did you drink enough milk as a child?" But it's my life-style, the sports I push myself into, whitewater rafting and stadium show jumping and backcountry skiing, the kinds of good times broken bones are made of.

Debra says it's because of my lover, but I was like this before he came along and I know it's something more basic than love. The only list that's longer than the things I've done is the list of things I've yet to do: kayak, hang glide, parachute; I think I want to learn how to fly.

Debra says, "Isn't it time for you to think about having a baby?"

"I am a dog mother," I say. "And I can still live my life."

"Yeah," Debra says. "Whatever that is."

I have always had a better relationship with Jackson than with Hailey. Part of it, I guess, is that you always love the problem child a little more, and part of it is the squeaky-wheel thing; Hailey is simply a low-maintenance dog. Jackson, on the other hand, is a charm machine. He has cost me over two thousand dollars in vet bills, I don't even keep track of the money that goes to the dogcatcher, and who gets all the treats? Just ask Hailey.

About once a month I have to go and bail Jackson out at the pound. I walk into the dark, urine-splattered corridor to find him resting comfortably, paws crossed. He's bullshitting with the malamute next to him. "What're you in for this time?" he's saying. "Dog at large, or something worth talking about?" He raises one furry eyebrow in my direction. "Hi, Mom," he says. "What kept you?"

Only once in Hailey's seven-year life has the dogcatcher picked her up for loitering at the end of my driveway and taken her to jail. I was in the bathtub when it happened, and she must have thought he was coming to visit us or she wouldn't have wiggled up to him, wouldn't have put that one fateful paw into the street. I was at the pound in minutes, and when I looked through the little glass window and I saw her and she saw me she made a noise like naked women burning in the fires of hell.

When my horse's hooves met and shattered the bones in my left forearm, I didn't see them coming. He was on the lunge line, we had just changed leads, and I was walking back to the center of the circle he would make around me. And then I was lying on the ground, my hand flopped over backwards, still connected to me by muscle and flesh and yet separate somehow. Not only the fractures of the eighteen or nineteen bone chips the doctors had to remove, but another separation, a detachment made necessary by pain. It was something not wholly mine anymore, like a child, like a lover, it was and was not my arm.

When the paramedics came and tried to pull my jacket off over my head, I asked them to please use a scissors. My jacket, my sweatshirt, my flannel shirt fell around me in strips.

"If they're in enough pain," the nurse with the scissors said, "they'll even let us cut their hair."

After the operation, after the implanting of the two steel plates, the fourteen screws, the piece of cadaver from the bone bank, my lover, the one whose favorite song was "Desperado," dedicated himself to me like a husband, like a mother, like a best friend. He cooked and cleaned and read to me and washed my hair in the bathtub.

He said, "I wish it could always be this way."

"Of course he does," Debra said. "You're helpless and he's in control."

It didn't last. My arm improved, as it was bound to.

I said, "Is there anything I could do, outside of shattering bones, that would make you treat me like this again?"

A few months later Jackson got arrested outside a shopping mall on an attacking dog charge. I was inside, trying on a dress for somebody else's wedding, when I heard the barking. By the time I got there, this was the scene: a screaming eight-year-old, his outraged father, a security guard with a billy club, Jackson in the pickup, wagging his tail and barking like a madman.

The outraged father said, "Your dog bit my son."

The security guard said, "Ma'am, you're lucky I didn't have a pistol, or your dog would be lying in a pool of blood."

I put Jackson on his leash and he sat like a statue at my feet. The cops came. One of them was a flirt. Nobody could find a mark on the little boy's hand, on either of his hands, and the little boy had forgotten which hand Jackson bit.

I showed them my rabies papers. The animal control officer said, "The dog will have to be impounded for ten days."

I said, "Even if he didn't bite anybody?"

He said, "Rabies is a very tricky disease."

He said, "It's ten dollars a day plus court costs, plus fines. At least a hundred and fifty for 'attacking dog.'"

The little boy was in the cop car making the lights go around.

A lady in a blue suit stopped to talk to Jackson. She surveyed the scene. Jackson looked at her as though he was Clark Gable. She leaned into the window of the cop car and said this:

"Little boy, what goes around comes around and one day a great big German shepherd is going to bite off your hand."

I told you, Jackson has that effect on people. The animal control officer led the lady in the blue suit away. He took Jackson's leash and asked him to jump into the big box on the back of his truck.

Jackson took one look over his shoulder at me and jumped. "Anything, Mom," he said, "anything, for a ride."

For the first time I noticed Hailey, curled quietly and almost asleep, on top of the spare tire in the back of my truck.

"Frankly," I said to Jackson, "this is getting a little old."

My friend Debra has a theory that women are the real male chauvinists. "You don't believe it," she says. "You should read more fairy tales. The man goes out and performs a heroic and spectacular deed, and the whole time the woman is at home waiting for him to return, to kiss and awaken her, waiting for her life to begin."

It's not the way I would say it, but I can't say she's entirely wrong.

In spite of that, I find a new lover. He is kinder, I'm guessing, than God. He is the type of man who knows that women have a secret, and even though he understands that he can't know what it is, he's smart enough to want to live in its light. To the best of my knowledge, he's never heard of the Eagles.

We plant a garden together, way too early in the season, not because we are ignorant about the weather, but because our need for a symbol outweighs our fear for the plants. On nights that threaten to freeze, we make paper hats for the tomatoes and peppers and our garden looks like a bunch of British navy men, buried to their eyes.

I want to tell Debra that he speaks only French when we make love, even though it's not true.

Okay. Because it's not true.

Debra says, "You need this right now."

But this affair is not what she thinks: good sex with a nice man.

It is a whole universe in there and I want to tell her I'm revising my list. Sky diving and hang gliding are gone. Babies, therefore, are higher.

Everything about sex, even the simplicity of an orgasm, seems to be made more complicated by all this gazing into each other's eyes. "High density" is the phrase I can't shake from my mind.

Afterwards, before sleep, with his body curled around mine, the only image I can hold on to is this:

Once when Jackson and I were hiking we found a cow, at least twenty days dead and bloated. Jackson tore its swollen belly open with his toenails and crawled inside its rib cage and wouldn't come out all that afternoon, all that night, and part of the next day.

It hits me in the morning as I'm taking the hats off of the tomatoes:

This is a kind of flying.

A Blizzard Under Blue Sky

The doctor said I was clinically depressed. It was February, the month in which depression runs rampant in the inversion-cloaked Salt Lake Valley and the city dwellers escape to Park City, where the snow is fresh and the sun is shining and everybody is happy, except me. In truth, my life was on the verge of more spectacular and satisfying discoveries than I had ever imagined, but of course I couldn't see that far ahead. What I saw was work that wasn't getting done, bills that weren't getting paid, and a man I'd given my heart to weekending in the desert with his ex.

The doctor said, "I can give you drugs."

I said, "No way."

She said, "The machine that drives you is broken. You need something to help you get it fixed."

I said, "Winter camping."

She said, "Whatever floats your boat."

One of the things I love the most about the natural world is the way it gives you what's good for you even if you don't know it at the time. I had never been winter camping before, at least not in the high country, and the weekend I chose to try and fix my machine was the same weekend the air mass they called the Alaska Clipper showed up. It was thirty-two degrees below zero in town on the night I spent in my snow cave. I don't know how cold it was out on Beaver Creek. I had listened to the weather forecast, and to the advice of my housemate, Alex, who was an experienced winter camper.

"I don't know what you think you're going to prove by freezing to death," Alex said, "but if you've got to go, take my bivvy sack; it's warmer than anything you have."

"Thanks," I said.

"If you mix Kool-Aid with your water it won't freeze up," he said, "and don't forget lighting paste for your stove."

"Okay," I said.

"I hope it turns out to be worth it," he said, "because you are going to freeze your butt."

When everything in your life is uncertain, there's nothing quite like the clarity and precision of fresh snow and blue sky. That was the first thought I had on Saturday morning as I stepped away from the warmth of my truck and let my skis slap the snow in front of me. There was no wind and no clouds that morning, just still air and cold sunshine. The hair in my nostrils froze almost immediately. When I took a deep breath, my lungs only filled up halfway.

I opened the tailgate to excited whines and whimpers. I never go skiing without Jackson and Hailey: my two best friends, my yin and yang of dogs. Some of you might know Jackson. He's the oversized sheepdog-and-something-else with the great big nose and the bark that will shatter glass. He

gets out and about more than I do. People I've never seen
before come by my house daily and call him by name. He's all
grace, and he's tireless; he won't go skiing with me unless I
let him lead. Hailey is not so graceful, and her body seems in
constant indecision when she runs. When we ski she stays
behind me, and on the downhills she tries to sneak rides on
my skis.

The dogs ran circles in the chest-high snow while I inven-
toried my backpack one more time to make sure I had everything I needed. My sleeping bag, my Thermarest, my stove,
Alex's bivvy sack, matches, lighting paste, flashlight, knife. I
brought three pairs of long underwear—tops and bottoms—
so I could change once before I went to bed, and once again in
the morning, so I wouldn't get chilled by my own sweat. I
brought paper and pen, and Kool-Aid to mix with my water. I
brought Mountain House chicken stew and some freeze-dried
green peas, some peanut butter and honey, lots of dried apricots, coffee and Carnation instant breakfast for morning.

Jackson stood very still while I adjusted his backpack. He
carries the dog food and enough water for all of us. He takes
himself very seriously when he's got his pack on. He won't
step off the trail for any reason, not even to chase rabbits, and
he gets nervous and angry if I do. That morning he was impatient with me. "Miles to go, Mom," he said over his shoulder.
I snapped my boots into my skis and we were off.

There are not too many good things you can say about
temperatures that dip past twenty below zero, except this:
They turn the landscape into a crystal palace and they turn
your vision into Superman's. In the cold thin morning air the
trees and mountains, even the twigs and shadows, seemed to
leap out of the background like a 3-D movie, only it was better
than 3-D because I could feel the sharpness of the air.

I have a friend in Moab who swears that Utah is the center of the fourth dimension, and although I know he has in mind something much different and more complicated than subzero weather, it was there, on that ice-edged morning, that I felt on the verge of seeing something more than depth perception in the brutal clarity of the morning sun.

As I kicked along the first couple of miles, I noticed the sun crawling higher in the sky and yet the day wasn't really warming, and I wondered if I should have brought another vest, another layer to put between me and the cold night ahead.

It was utterly quiet out there, and what minimal noise we made intruded on the morning like a brass band: the squeaking of my bindings, the slosh of the water in Jackson's pack, the whoosh of nylon, the jangle of dog tags. It was the bass line and percussion to some primal song, and I kept wanting to sing to it, but I didn't know the words.

Jackson and I crested the top of a hill and stopped to wait for Hailey. The trail stretched out as far as we could see into the meadow below us and beyond, a double track and pole plants carving though softer trails of rabbit and deer.

"Nice place," I said to Jackson, and his tail thumped the snow underneath him without sound.

We stopped for lunch near something that looked like it could be a lake in its other life, or maybe just a womb-shaped meadow. I made peanut butter and honey sandwiches for all of us, and we opened the apricots.

"It's fabulous here," I told the dogs. "But so far it's not working."

There had never been anything wrong with my life that a few good days in the wilderness wouldn't cure, but there I sat in the middle of all those crystal-coated trees, all that diamond-studded sunshine, and I didn't feel any better. Apparently clinical depression was not like having a bad day, it wasn't even like having a lot of bad days, it was more like a house of mirrors, it was like being in a room full of one-way glass.

"Come on, Mom," Jackson said. "Ski harder, go faster, climb higher."

Hailey turned her belly to the sun and groaned.

"He's right," I told her. "It's all we can do."

After lunch the sun had moved behind our backs, throwing a whole different light on the path ahead of us. The snow we moved through stopped being simply white and became translucent, hinting at other colors, reflections of blues and purples and grays. I thought of Moby Dick, you know, the whiteness of the whale, where white is really the absence of all color, and whiteness equals truth, and Ahab's search is finally futile, as he finds nothing but his own reflection.

"Put your mind where your skis are," Jackson said, and we made considerably better time after that.

The sun was getting quite low in the sky when I asked Jackson if he thought we should stop to build the snow cave, and he said he'd look for the next good bank. About one hundred yards down the trail we found it, a gentle slope with eastern exposure that didn't look like it would cave in under any circumstances. Jackson started to dig first.

Let me make one thing clear. I knew only slightly more about building snow caves than Jackson, having never built one, and all my knowledge coming from disaster tales of winter camping fatalities. I knew several things *not* to do when building a snow cave, but I was having a hard time knowing what exactly to do. But Jackson helped, and Hailey supervised, and before too long we had a little cave built, just big enough for three. We ate dinner quite pleased with our accomplishments and set the bivvy sack up inside the cave just as the sun slipped away and dusk came over Beaver Creek.

The temperature, which hadn't exactly soared during the day, dropped twenty degrees in as many minutes, and suddenly it didn't seem like such a great idea to change my long underwear. The original plan was to sleep with the dogs inside the bivvy sack but outside the sleeping bag, which was okay with Jackson the super-metabolizer, but not so with Hailey, the couch potato. She whined and wriggled and managed to stuff her entire fat body down inside my mummy bag, and Jackson stretched out full-length on top.

One of the unfortunate things about winter camping is that it has to happen when the days are so short. Fourteen hours is a long time to lie in a snow cave under the most perfect of circumstances. And when it's thirty-two below, or forty, fourteen hours seems like weeks.

I wish I could tell you I dropped right off to sleep. In truth, fear crept into my spine with the cold and I never closed my eyes. Cuddled there, amid my dogs and water bottles, I spent half of the night chastising myself for thinking I was Wonder Woman, not only risking my own life but the lives of my dogs, and the other half trying to keep the numbness in my feet from crawling up to my knees. When I did doze off, which was actually more like blacking out than dozing off, I'd come back to my senses wondering if I had frozen to death, but the alternating pain and numbness that started in my extremities and worked its way into my bones convinced me I must still be alive.

It was a clear night, and every now and again I would poke my head out of its nest of down and nylon to watch the progress of the moon across the sky. There is no doubt that it was the longest and most uncomfortable night of my life.

But then the sky began to get gray, and then it began to get pink, and before too long the sun was on my bivvy sack, not warm, exactly, but holding the promise of warmth later in the day. And I ate apricots and drank Kool-Aid-flavored coffee and celebrated the rebirth of my fingers and toes, and the survival of many more important parts of my body. I sang "Rocky Mountain High" and "If I Had a Hammer," and yodeled and whistled, and even danced the two-step with Jackson and let him lick my face. And when Hailey finally emerged from the sleeping bag a full hour after I did, we shared a peanut butter and honey sandwich and she said nothing ever tasted so good.

We broke camp and packed up and kicked in the snow cave with something resembling glee.

I was five miles down the trail before I realized what had happened. Not once in that fourteen-hour night did I think about deadlines, or bills, or the man in the desert. For the first time in many months I was happy to see a day beginning. The morning sunshine was like a present from the gods. What really happened, of course, is that I remembered about joy.

I know that one night out at thirty-two below doesn't sound like much to those of you who have climbed Everest or run the Iditarod or kayaked to Antarctica, and I won't try to convince you that my life was like the movies where depression goes away in one weekend, and all of life's problems vanish with a moment's clear sight. The simple truth of the matter is this: On Sunday I had a glimpse outside of the house of mirrors, on Saturday I couldn't have seen my way out of a paper bag. And while I was skiing back toward the truck that morning, a wind came up behind us and swirled the snow around our bodies like a blizzard under blue sky. And I was struck by the simple perfection of the snowflakes, and startled by the hopefulness of sun on frozen trees.

Sometimes You Talk About Idaho

You've come, finally, to a safe place. It could be labeled *safe place*, marquee-style in bright glittering letters. You've put the time in to get there. You've read all the books. You have cooked yourself elaborate gourmet meals. You have brought home fresh-cut flowers. You love your work. You love your friends. It's the single life in the high desert. No booze, no drugs. It isn't just something you tell yourself. It's something you believe.

The man you admire most in the world calls you and asks you out to lunch. He is your good father, the one you trust, the one you depend on. The only one, besides your agent and the editors, who still sees your work.

You have lunch with him often because he is honest and rare, and because he brings a certain manic energy to your life. He is the meter of your own authenticity, the way his eyes drop when you say even the most marginally ingenuous thing.

He lives in a space you can only pretend to imagine. When he talks about his own life there seem to be no participants and no events, just a lot of energy moving and spinning and changing hands. It's dizzying, really; sex becomes religion, and religion becomes art.

Sometimes you talk about Idaho: the smell of spruce trees, the snap of a campfire, the arc of a dry fly before it breaks the surface of the water. Idaho is something he can speak about concretely.

He always asks about your love life. No, you say, there's no one at all.

"The problem," he says, "with living alone is that you have to go so far away to the place you can do your work, and when you're finished there's no one there to tell you whether or not you've gotten back."

Your good father smiles a smile of slight embarrassment which is as uncomfortable as new shoes on his soft face. He has a friend, he says, that he'd like you to meet.

"He is both smart and very masculine," your good father says, something in his voice acknowledging that this is a rare combination because he wants you to know he's on your side here. "Our friendship," he says, "is ever new.

"Imagine a first date," your good father says, "where you don't have to watch your vocabulary. Imagine a man," he says, "who might be as intense as you."

Your good father's friend lives in Manhattan, twenty-two hundred miles from the place you've learned to call home. He's a poet, a concert pianist, a soap opera star. He's translated plays from five different Native American languages. He's an environmentalist, a humanist, he's hard to the left.

"He's been through a lot of self-evaluation. He wants a relationship," your good father says, "and he's a dog person.

Now that you fly back to New York so often, it could be just the right thing."

You watch him wait for your reaction. You look at the lines that pain has made on his face and realize that you love your good father more than anyone you have slept with in the last five years. You would do anything he told you to do.

"Sounds like fun," you say, without blinking. You are pure nonchalance. A relationship, you've decided, is not something you need like a drug, but a journey, a circumstance, a choice you might make on a particular day.

"My friend loves the mountains, and the desert," your good father says. "He comes out here as often as he can. His real name is Evan, but he's played the same part on the soap for so many years now, everyone we know just calls him Tex."

"Tex?" you say.

"I didn't tell you," he says. "My friend plays a cowboy." Your good father smiles his embarrassed smile. "That's the best part."

You fly to the East Coast on an enormous plane that is mostly empty. You watch the contours of the land get steadily greener, badlands to prairies to cornfields, till the clouds close your view and water runs off the wing.

Somehow you have lived to be twenty-nine years old without ever having gone on a blind date. You don't let yourself admit it, but you are excited beyond words.

You let your mother dress you. She lives in New Jersey and is an actress and you think it's her privilege. She makes you do the following things you are not accustomed to doing: wear foundation, curl your eyelashes, part your hair on the side. Even the Mona Lisa, she says, doesn't look pretty with her hair parted in the middle. She gives you her car so you don't have to take the bus into New York, and in exchange you leave her a phone number where she can reach you. She promises not to call.

It's a little dislocating in New Jersey, where there are cars on the road at all hours and it never really gets dark at night. On the freeway, four miles outside of Newark, you see a deer walking across a cement overpass that's been planted with trees. This seems more amazing to you than it probably is. A sign from your homeland, safe passage, good luck.

It works. You make it through the improbable fact of the Lincoln Tunnel and it doesn't cave in. You find a twenty-four-hour garage four blocks from Moran's Seafood, the meeting place for your date. On the way there you see a woman who looks very happy carrying a starfish in a translucent Tupperware bowl. You only have to walk down one street that scares you a little bit. You get to the restaurant first, and your wide-eyed reflection in the glass behind the bar startles you a little. You resist the urge to tell the bartender that you have a blind date.

When he walks in the door there's no mistaking him. He's the soap opera star with the umbrella, the strong back and shoulders, the laugh lines America loves. As he scans the bar it occurs to you for the first time to wonder what kind of a sales job your good father has done on him about you. Then you are shaking hands, then he is picking up your umbrella, one arm hooked in yours guiding you to the table for two.

It is only awkward for the first ten minutes. He is a great mass of charisma moving forward to ever more entertaining subjects. You are both so conscious of keeping the conversation going that you don't look at the menu till the waiter has come back for the fifth time.

Of all the things on the menu, you pick the only one that's

difficult to pronounce. You have just passed a fluency exam in French that is one of the requirements of your Ph.D., but saying *en papillote* to the waiter is something that is beyond your power to do. So you describe the dish in English and when the waiter has watched you suffer to his satisfaction, he moves his pen and nods his head.

During dinner, you cover all the required topics for first dates in the nineties: substance abuse, failed marriage, hopes, dreams, and aspirations. You talk about your dogs so much he gets confused and thinks they are your children. He uses emotion words when he talks, sometimes more than one in a sentence: *ache, frightened, rapture.* And something else: He is listening, not only to the words you are saying, but to your rhythms, your reverberations, he picks them up like a machine. Something in his manner is so much like your good father that a confusion which is not altogether unpleasant settles in behind your heart.

Between the herbal tea and the triple fudge decadence he's ordered so that you can have one bite, he reaches across the table and takes your hand in both of his. Then he calls you a swell critter.

You feel a hairline fracture easing through your structure the way snow separates before an avalanche on a too-warm winter day. Something in the air smells a little like salvation, and you breathe deeper every minute but you can't fill your lungs. When all the tables are empty and every restaurant employee is staring at you in disgust, you finally let go of his hand.

Then you go walking. One end of Chelsea to the other, all the time circumventing the block with your garage. He knows about the architecture. He reads from the historic plaques. He shows you nooks and crannies, hidden doorways, remnants of the Latinate style.

It's been raining softly for the hours since dinner and you can feel your hair creeping back over to its comfortable middle part. You smile at him like the Mona Lisa, and he looks as though he's going to kiss you, but doesn't. Then the sky opens up and you duck into a café for more herbal tea.

The café is crowded and the streets are full of people and it makes no sense to you when he tells you it's three o'clock in the morning. You can't possibly, he says, drive all the way back to New Jersey tonight. It's your first real chance to size him up and you do. From the empty next table your good father gives you a wink. "It would be foolish," you say, "to drive in the middle of the night."

When you look back on this date it's the cab ride you'll remember. Broadway going by in a wild blur of green lights, the tallest buildings all lit up like daytime. Your driver and another in a cab next to yours hang heads out their windows and converse at fifty miles an hour in a tongue that sounds a little like Portuguese, a little like music. It's pure unburdened anticipation: you both know sex is imminent, but you don't yet hold the fact of it in your hand. You are laughing and leaning against him. You are watching yourself on the giant screen, western woman finds daytime cowboy in the big city, where even if it wasn't raining, you couldn't see a single star.

His building is a West Side co-op, a name that sounds happy to you, like a place where everyone should get along. In his apartment there are the black-and-white photos you expected, the vertical blinds, the tiny kitchen and immense workplace, the antique rolltop desk.

Some tea without caffeine? he says. And you nod. You count. This is your eleventh cup of herbal tea today. You have never done a first date without alcohol. Now you know why.

You watch him move around the room like a soap opera star. Take one: western woman's seduction: a smile, a touch, a glance. You're still waiting for the big one-liner when he starts kissing you, his hand cupped around your chin, one on the back of your head. Procter and Gamble Industries has taught him how to do this. "Slowly now," the director says, "a little softer. Turn the chin, turn the chin, we can't see her face." You aren't fooling anybody. It's way better than TV.

"Let's forget the herbal tea," he says, which is a disappointment. You want to see the script. You want to make a big red X over that line and write in another, but he has your hand and is leading you to the bedroom with the queen-size bed and the wrought-iron headboard with the sunset over the mountains and there are so many things to think about. Like how many days since your last period and the percentage of people in New York with AIDS, and what you can say to make him realize, if it matters anymore, that going to bed on first dates is not something you do with great regularity. Something needs to be said here, not exactly to defend your virtue, but to make it clear that the act needs to be meaningful, to make it matter, not for all time or forever but for right now, because that's what you've decided it needs to be with sex—after discarding all those other requirements over the years—something that matters right now.

"I'm feeling a little strange," you begin, and you realize this isn't just about you but you're testing him to see if he'll let you talk. "I seem to be violating my own code of dating," you say. "If I have one, that is. I mean, I wanted to come here with you, I didn't want this to end just now, and then we have this other person in common, and because we both love him, there's this closeness between us, this trust which may be totally inappropriate, and so," you wind up, "I'm just feeling a little strange."

This is what happens, you realize, when you begin to get

mentally healthy. Instead of letting yourself be whisked silently off to bed you feel compelled to say a lot of mostly incoherent things in run-on sentences.

"I know how you feel," he says. "Me too. But I want this closeness. I don't want you to go back home without us having had it."

It's not exactly a declaration, but it's good enough for you. You fall into the ocean that banks the sunset over mountains. It's a thunderstorm in the desert. It's warm wind on snow. You lose count of orgasms under the smoky city lighting, first streetlight and then daylight, the contours always changing.

"Having fun?" he says, at one point or another. And you nod because fun is one of the things you are having.

He does something to the back of your neck that is closer, more intimate, somehow, even than having him inside you. You read an article once on craniosacral massage, where the body's task of pumping blood to the brain is performed by another person, giving the patient's body the closest thing it's ever had to total rest.

At eight-thirty your mother calls and you take a break long enough to mumble a few words into the phone. "I'm perfectly safe," you tell her, and laugh all the way back to the bedroom at the absurdity of your lie.

It is noon before you emerge, still not having slept, your body feeling numb and tingling and drenched, weightless, rain-soaked, rejuvenated.

But like it or not, it's the next day. You both have appointments. He kisses you twice. "Dinner?" he says. "It'll be late," you say. "That's okay," he says, "call me."

You go to meeting after meeting, and finally to a party with people who mean everything to your career. You are wearing the same clothes as yesterday, walking a little tender, and

bowlegged as a bear. Your editor, by some miracle of perception, takes your hand and doesn't let it go all night, even when
you are involved in two separate conversations.

Later, you call the soap opera star. He tries to give you
directions. "You," he says, "are on the East Side. I am on the
West Side."

You tell him you've been to New York before. You hang
up.

On the way to his house you get lost. It is raining the kind
of rain it never rains in the high desert. A saturating rain
where the air spaces between the raindrops contain almost as
much moisture as the raindrops themselves. You drive your
mother's car through running canals deeper than your wheel
wells. You have never been to this part of Manhattan before.
Street after street bears a name you don't recognize. Dark
figures loom in dark doorways, and the same series of parks
seems to have you boxed in. Your defroster can't keep up with
your anxiety. Then suddenly you are back on Broadway. You
find his house.

"I had a learning experience," you say. What should have
taken fifteen minutes has taken an hour and a half. He isn't
angry, but he takes the keys from your hand. Together you
look for an open garage.

"Dinner?" he says. You shake your head either no you
haven't had it or no you don't want it.

"If you're not sleeping," he says, "you need to eat." The
two of you look like war-zone survivors. You both try to be
charming and fail. Even the simplest conversation is beyond
your power. Finally you eat in silence. You fall into bed. It's
sleep you both need, but there's the fact of what's insatiable
between you. All night you keep reaching, tumbling, waiting
for the bell to ring to let you know you've found each other, to
let you know it's okay to sleep.

In what seems like minutes, it's time to say goodbye, way too early, not even light out, dusky gray New York morning, clear or cloudy, who can tell without the stars? He has to go to the studio and put on his cowboy boots and court somebody named Hannah, so that all of America can sigh.

"So is Tex nice?" you say, sleepy-eyed as he kisses you goodbye.

"Darlin'," he says, "they don't come any nicer than Tex. Drop the keys in the mail slot. Take care."

When he's gone the phone rings and the machine gets it. Past experience has taught you to expect a woman's voice, but it's your good father, wanting Evan to tell him how everything went. You imagine your good father in the desert, bright sunshine, sage and warm wind. When you hear his laugh crackle over the answering machine your dislocation is complete.

You wander around New York until your lunch date. One of the polished magazines you have written a few short pieces for wants to send you to Yugoslavia. This is not something you can immediately comprehend. They keep talking about it, airfare and train passes and what time of year is the most beautiful, and even though they have said they want you to go you keep thinking, But why are they saying this to me?

It's Wednesday, a matinee day, so you stand in line to get half-priced tickets to a musical, even though you prefer drama, but you know you aren't up for anything that requires you to think. You pick the wrong musical anyway. The first words delivered onstage are "Love changes everything," and it's downhill from there. You leave feeling like you've been through three and a half hours of breath work. On the way up Fifty-seventh Street you realize a valuable and frightening thing: Today you want to be in love more than you want anything; the National Book Award, say, or a Pulitzer Prize.

You've left something at the soap opera star's apartment; a

contact lens, a computer disk, your forty-dollar Oscar de la Renta underwear. It takes several phone calls to determine a time to retrieve them. He is short on the phone, on the other line to a director in London, and you realize you've stepped across some kind of a boundary into his space. You have forgotten how New Yorkers can be about their space. You are overly hard on yourself. Where you live, there is plenty of space. There is so much goddam space you can hardly believe it. Finally, it's the doorman who lets you into his empty apartment.

And then you go home, on another enormous airplane, and sit next to a fat woman who is reading a book called *Why Women Confuse Love with Sex*. It's not her you're mad at, but you glare at her so she won't speak to you because you know that anything—anything—anybody says to you will make you cry and cry.

For two days you catch up on sleep and expect him to call. On the third day you come to your senses enough to go hiking, to get out into the landscape that heals you. There is a dynamic in the desert that you understand perfectly: the dry, dry earth and the plants designed to live almost forever without the simple and basic ingredients they need the most. After five days you know he isn't going to call, which is okay, because out of the rubble you carried back from the city you have resurrected your independence. Your work surrounds you like a featherbed and things almost go back to how they were before. But now desire grows inside you like a plant, a big green leafy thing that has been fed only once, but now that it's growing, it won't be still. You sit in your own house and talk to your dogs. More often than not, you answer back.

Your good father calls and asks you out to breakfast. It's an early appointment but you get up even earlier to bathe and dress. It's breakfast at Howard Johnson's but you wear what you wore at Moran's. You even curl your eyelashes. You tell your good father that Evan was everything he said he would be. You run down the weekend with more facts than innuendo. He gets the picture. He is, he says, a lonely man himself.

You tell him about the leafy thing in your stomach, how you have detached it from Evan, how your desire has become something you own, after all. When you get to that part, tears spring into your eyes. It's your turn to give the performance, and its authenticity doesn't make it any less theatrical. It's honesty you are striving for, and still, you're a little bigger than life. Your good father's eyes tell you you've succeeded, and yet your motives are too suspect for even you to explore. You choose to boil it down to what's simple: You perform for your good father because you love him. Anything else is beside the point. Your good father reaches across the table and takes your hand in both of his. "Evan will call you," he says. "I know him. He will."

You wonder what Evan has said to your good father on the phone. You wonder why there's no word for the opposite of lonely. You wonder if there's a difference between whatever might be truth and a performance that isn't a lie. In your life right now, you can't find one.

Symphony

_ _ _ _ _ _ _ _ _ _ _

Sometimes life is ridiculously simple. I lost fifteen pounds and the men want me again. I can see it in the way they follow my movements, not just with their eyes but with their whole bodies, the way they lean into me until they almost topple over, the way they always seem to have itches on the ba f their necks. And I'll admit this: I am collecting them like gold-plated sugar spoons, one from every state.

This is a difficult story to tell because what's right about what I have to say is only as wide as a tightrope, and what's wrong about it yawns wide, beckoning, on either side. I have always said I have no narcotic, smiling sadly at stories of ruined lives, safely remote from the twelve-step program and little red leather booklets that say "One Day at a Time." But there is something so sweet about the first kiss, the first surrender that, like the words "I want you," can never mean precisely the same thing again. It is delicious and addicting. It is, I'm guessing, the most delicious thing of all.

There are a few men who matter, and by writing them down in this story I can make them seem like they have an order, or a sequence, or a priority, because those are the kinds of choices that language forces upon us, but language can't touch the joyful and slightly disconcerting feeling of being very much in love, but not knowing exactly with whom.

First I will tell you about Phillip, who is vast and dangerous, his desires uncontainable and huge. He is far too talented, a grown-up tragedy of a gifted child, massively in demand. He dances, he weaves, he writes a letter that could wring light from a black hole. He has mined gold in the Yukon, bonefished in Belize. He has crossed Iceland on a dogsled, he is the smartest man that all his friends know. His apartment smells like wheat bread, cooling. His body smells like spice. Sensitive and scared scared scared of never becoming a father, he lives in New York City and is very careful about his space. It is easy to confuse what he has learned to do in bed for love or passion or art, but he is simply a master craftsman, and very proud of his good work.

Christopher is innocent. Very young and wide-open. He's had good mothering and no father to make him afraid to talk about his heart. In Nevada he holds hands with middle-aged women while the underground tests explode beneath them. He studies marine biology, acting, and poetry, and is not yet quite aware of his classic good looks. Soon someone will tell him, but it won't be me. A few years ago he said in a few more years he'd be old enough for me, and in a few more years, it will be true. For now we are friends and I tell him my system, how I have learned to get what I want from many sources, and none. He says this: You are a complicated woman. Even when you say you don't want anything, you want more than that.

I have a dream in which a man becomes a wolf. He is sleeping, cocooned, and when he stretches and breaks the parchment there are tufts of hair across his back and shoulders, and on the backs of his hands. It is Christopher, I suspect, though I can't see his face. When I wake up I am in Phillip's bed. My back is to his side and yet we are touching at all the pressure points. In the predawn I can see the line of electricity we make, a glow like neon, the curve of a wooden instrument. As I wake, "Symphony" is the first word that forms in my head.

Jonathan came here from the Okavango Delta in Botswana; he's tall and hairy and clever and strong. In my living room I watch him reach inside his shirt and scratch his shoulder. It is a savage movement, rangy and impatient, lazy too, and without a bit of self-consciousness. He is not altogether human. He has spent the last three years in the bush. I cook him T-bone steaks because he says he won't eat complicated food. He is skeptical of the hibachi, of the barely glowing coals. Where he comes from, they cook everything with fire. He says things against my ear, the names of places: Makgadikgadi Pans, Nxamaseri, Mpandamatenga, Gabarone. Say these words out loud and see what happens to you. Mosi-oa-Toenja, "The Smoke That Thunders." Look at the pictures: a rank of impalas slaking their thirst, giraffes, their necks entwined, a young bull elephant rising from the Chobe River. When I am with Jonathan I have this thought which delights and frightens me: It has been the animals that have attracted me all along. Not the cowboys, but the horses that carried them. Not the hunters, but the caribou and the bighorn. Not Jonathan, in his infinite loveliness, but the hippos, the kudu, and the big African cats. You fall in love with a man's animal spirit, Jonathan tells me, and then when he speaks like a human being, you don't know who he is.

There's one man I won't talk about, not because he is married, but because he is sacred. When he writes love letters to me he addresses them "my dear" and signs them with the first letter of his first name and one long black line. We have only made love one time. I will tell you only the one thing that must be told: After the only part of him I will ever hold collapsed inside me he said, "You are so incredibly gentle." It was the closest I have ever come to touching true love.

Another dream: I am in the house of my childhood, and I see myself, at age five, at the breakfast table; pancakes and sausage, my father in his tennis whites. The me that is dreaming, the older me, kneels down and holds out her arms waiting for the younger me to come and be embraced. Jonathan's arms twitch around me and I am suddenly awake inside a body, inside a world where it has become impossible to kneel down and hold out my arms. Still sleeping, Jonathan pulls my hand across his shoulder, and presses it hard against his face.

I'm afraid of what you might be thinking. That I am a certain kind of person, and that you are the kind of person who knows more about my story than me. But you should know this: I could love any one of them, in an instant and with every piece of my heart, but none of them nor the world will allow it, and so I move between them, on snowy highways and crowded airplanes. I was in New York this morning. I woke up in Phillip's bed. Come here, he's in my hair. You can smell him.

In My Next Life

— — — — — — — — — — —

This is a love story. Although Abby and I were never lovers. That's an odd thing for me to have to say about another woman, because I've never had a woman lover, and yet with Abby it would have been possible. Of course with Abby anything was possible, and I often wonder if she hadn't gotten sick if we would have been lovers: one day our holding and touching and hugging slipping quietly into something more. It would have been beside the point and redundant, our lovemaking, but it might have been wonderful all the same.

That was the summer I was organic gardening for a living, and I had a small but steady clientele who came to me for their produce and kept me financially afloat. I had a trade going with Carver's Bakery, tomatoes for bread, and another with the farmers' market in Salt Lake City, fresh herbs for chicken and groceries. I grew wheat grass for my landlord Thomas and his lover, who both had AIDS. I traded Larry, at the Purina Mill, all the corn his kids could eat for all the grain I needed for my mare. She was half wild and the other half stubborn, and I should have turned her out to pasture like most of my friends said, or shot her like the rest recommended, but I had an idea that she and I could be great together if we ever both felt good on the same day.

Abby had long black hair she wore in a single braid and eyes the color of polished jade. Her shoulders were rounded like a swimmer's, although she was afraid of the water, and her hands were quick and graceful and yet seemed to be capable of incredible strength.

I met her at a horse-handling clinic she was teaching in Salt Lake that I'd gone to with my crazy mare.

"There are no problem horses," Abby said. "Someone has taught her to be that way."

In the middle of explaining to her that it wasn't me who taught my horse her bad habits, I realized it could have been. Abby had a way of looking at me, of looking into me, that made everything I said seem like the opposite of the truth.

"There are three things to remember when working with horses," Abby said to the women who had gathered for the class. "Ask, Receive, Give." She said each word slowly, and separated them by breaths. "Now what could be simpler than that?"

I rode as hard as I knew how that day at the clinic. Abby was calm, certain, full of images. "Your arms and hands are running water," she said. "Let the water pour over your horse. Let the buttons on your shirt come undone. Let your body melt like ice cream and dribble out the bottom of your bones."

My mare responded to the combination of my signals and Abby's words. She was moving with confidence, bending underneath me, her back rounded, her rhythm steady and strong.

"Catch the energy as if you were cradling a baby." Abby said. "Grow your fingers out to the sky. Fly with your horse. Feel that you are dancing." She turned from one woman to another. "Appeal to the great spirit," she said. "Become aware, inhibit, allow."

At the end of the day while we were walking out the horses Abby said, "You are a lovely, lovely woman. Tell me what else you do."

I told her I played the banjo, which was the other thing I was doing at the time, with a group that was only marginally popular with people my age but a big hit with the older folks in the Fallen Arches Square Dance Club.

Abby told me she had always been intimidated by musicians.

She told me I had medieval hair.

On the first day after the clinic that Abby and I spent together I told her that meeting her was going to change my whole life. She seemed neither threatened nor surprised by this information; if anything, she was mildly pleased. "Life gives us what we need when we need it," she said. "Receiving what it gives us is a whole other thing."

We were both involved with unavailable men, one by drugs, one by alcohol, both by nature. There were some differences. She lived with her boyfriend, whose name was Roy. I lived alone. Roy was kind, at least, and faithful, and my man, whose name was Hardin, was not.

I said to Thomas, "I have met a woman who, if she were a man, I would be in love with." But of course Abby could have never been a man, and I fell in love anyway. It's not the kind

of definition Abby would have gotten mired in, but I think she
may also have been a little in love with me.

Once, on the phone, when we weren't sure if the conversation was over, when we weren't sure if we had actually said
goodbye, we both held our receivers, breathing silently, till
finally she had the guts to say, "Are you still there?

"We are a couple of silly women," she said, when we had
finally stopped laughing. "A couple of silly women who want
so badly to be friends."

Although only one-sixteenth Cherokee, and even that un-
documented, Abby was a believer in Native American medicine. Shamanic healing, specifically, is what she practiced.
The healing involved in shamanic work happens in mind jour-
neys a patient takes with the aid of a continuous drumbeat,
into the lower or upper world, accompanied by his or her
power animal. The power animal serves as the patient's inter-
preter, guardian, and all number of other things. The animals
take pity on us, it is believed, because of the confusion with
which we surround ourselves. The learning takes place in the
energy field where the animal and the human being meet.

A guided tour into the lower world with a buffalo is not the
kind of thing a white girl from New Jersey would discover on
her own, but for me, everything that came from Abby's mouth
was magic. If she had told me the world was flat, I'd have
found a way to make it true.

When Abby taught me the methods of shamanic healing I
started to try to journey too. Abby played the drum for me.
She shook the rattle around my body and blew power into my
breastbone and into the top of my skull. The drumming al-
tered my mental state, that was for certain, but I couldn't
make myself see anything I could define. If I pressed my arm
hard enough against my eyeballs I could start to see light

— — — — — — — — — — — — —

swirling. But a tunnel? another world? Animals and spirits I couldn't muster.

"People have different amounts of spiritual potential," she said, "and for some people it takes a while. Don't be discouraged by a slow start."

So I would try again and again to make forms out of the shapes inside my eyelids, and I'd stretch the truth of what I saw in the reporting. I wanted to go all of the places that Abby could go. I was afraid she might find another friend with more spiritual potential than me.

"You're seeing in a way you've never seen before," Abby said. "You just don't know how to recognize it. It isn't like cartoons on your eyelids. It's not like a big-screen TV."

Finally, my mind would make logical connections out of the things I was seeing. "It was a bear," I would say, "running away and then returning." Abby's green eyes never let mine falter. "A big white bear that could run on two legs." As I said the words, it seemed, I made it so. "It was turning somersaults, too, and rolling in the blueberries." It didn't feel like I was lying, but it also didn't feel like the truth.

One thing was certain. I believed what Abby saw. If she said she rose into the stars and followed them to South Africa, if she danced on the rooftops of Paris with her ancestors, if she and her power animal made love in the Siberian snow, I believed her. I still believe her. Abby didn't lie.

But it wasn't only the magic. Abby was gentle and funny and talked mostly with her hands. She made great mashed potatoes. She had advanced degrees in botany, biology, and art history. And the horses, Abby loved her horses more than any power animal her imagination could conjure up.

"The Indians don't believe in imagination," she told me. "They don't even have a word for it. Once you understand that fully this all becomes much easier."

We had climbed the mountain behind my house, way above the silver mine, and were lying in a meadow the moon made bright. Abby threw handfuls of cornmeal on the ground. "I'm feeding my power animal," she said. "When I do this he knows that I need him around."

I made Abby batches of fresh salsa, pesto, and spaghetti sauce. I brought her squash blossoms, red peppers, and Indian corn to make a necklace her power animal told her to wear.

She told me about her college roommate, Tracy, her best friend, she said, before me. Tracy's marriage had broken up, she said, because Tracy had been having an affair with a woman, and her husband, Steve, couldn't handle it. They had tried going to therapy together, but Tracy eventually chose the woman over Steve.

"She said she never expected to have an affair with a woman," Abby said, "but then they just fell in love."

I thought about my friend Thomas, about how he gets so angry whenever anybody says that they respect his sexual choice. "Choice has nothing to do with it," I can hear him saying. "Why would I ever have done this if I had had a choice?"

But I wonder if it's not a question of choice for a woman. Aren't there women who wake up tired of trying to bridge the unbridgeable gap, who wake up ready to hold and be held by somebody who knows what it means?

"In my next life," Thomas was famous for saying, "I'm coming back as a lesbian."

"That's what I did," my friend of five years, Joanne, said, when I asked her opinion, as if her lesbian affair was something I'd known about all along, "with Isabelle. And it was wonderful, for a while. But what happens too often is that somewhere down the line you are attracted to a man and want to go back, and then it's a whole new kind of guilt to deal with. You're hurting somebody who's on your team, who really knows you, who really is you, I suppose, if you stop and think."

"There are so many more interesting things to do than fall in love," Abby said. "If Roy and I split up, I want to live in a house full of women, old women and young women, teenagers and babies. Doesn't falling in love sound boring, compared to that?"

I had to admit, it didn't. We were both fighting our way out of codependency. I wasn't as far as she was yet.

"The problem with codependency," Abby said, "is that what you have to do to be codependent, and what you have to do to not be codependent, turn out so often to be the same thing."

"So what would you do about sex, in this house full of women?" I said. We were sitting sideways on her sofa like kids on a Flexible Flyer. She was braiding and unbraiding my medieval hair.

"Frankly," she said, "that's the least of my concerns."

"That's what you say now," I said, "but I think after a few years without, you would start to feel differently."

"Yeah, maybe you're right," she said, giving the short hairs at the nape of my neck a tug. "Maybe sex would turn out to be the big snafu."

It was only the third or fourth time we were together when Abby told me about the lump in her breast. "It's been there a long time," she said, "about two years, I guess, but my power animal says it's not cancer, and besides it gets bigger and smaller with my period. Cancer never does that."

Even the doctor, when she finally did go, said he was ninety-nine percent sure that the lump was not a "malignancy" (doctors apparently had stopped using the "C" word), but he wanted to take it out anyway, just to make sure.

On the night before Abby's biopsy, I made her favorite thing: three kinds of baked squash, butternut, buttercup, and acorn.

"Sometimes I'm jealous of Hardin," I said. "He lives right on the surface and he's happy there. Who am I to tell him how to live his life? I should be that happy in all my depth."

"I had a friend in grade school named Margaret Hitzrot," Abby said. "Once on our way to a day of skiing we were the first car in a twenty-one-vehicle pile up. Our car spun to a stop, unharmed against the snowbank, but facing back the way we had come, and we watched station wagons, delivery trucks, VW buses, collide and crash, spin and smash together. Mrs. Hitzrot said, 'Margaret, do you think we should wait for the police?' And Margaret said, 'If we don't get to the ski area before the lift opens the whole day will be ruined,' so we got in our car and drove away."

"It's not the worst way to live," I said.

"The problem with the surface," Abby said, "is that it's so slippery. Once you get bumped off, it's impossible to climb back on."

Abby's arms bore scars on the white underside, nearly up to the elbows, thin and delicate, like an oriental script. "It was a long, long time ago," she said. "And I wasn't trying to kill myself either. My stepfather had some serious problems. There was a good bit of sexual abuse. I never even thought about dying. I just wanted to make myself bleed."

After dinner we rode the horses up to our favorite meadow.

She had been riding my horse, who had turned to putty in her hands. I was riding one of hers, a big gray gelding who was honest as a stone. We kept saying we were going to switch back, now that my horse had been gentled, but I didn't push the issue. I was afraid my mare would go back to her old habits and Abby would be disappointed. It was something I'd never felt with a woman, this giant fear of looking bad.

I was depressed that night. Hardin was in another state with another woman, and it made me so mad that I cared.

"You have given all your power away to Hardin," Abby said. "You need to do something to get it back."

We sat under the star-filled sky and Abby said she would journey beside me, journey, she said, on my behalf. This was accomplished by our lying on the ground side by side. We touched at the shoulders, the knees, and the hips. We both tied bandannas around our heads, and Abby pulled her Walkman and drumming tape out of the saddlebags.

"Don't feel like you need to journey," she said. "I'll do all the work for you, but if you feel yourself slipping into a journey, go ahead and let it happen."

For a long time I watched the white spots turn on the inside of my bandanna while Abby's breathing quickened, and leveled and slowed. Then I saw a steady light, and reflections below it. It was my first real vision, nothing about it questionable or subject to change. It was moonlight over granite, I think, something shiny, and permanent and hard.

Abby came back slowly, and I turned off the tape.

"Your power source is the moon," she said. "It was a bear who told me. A giant bear that kept getting smaller and smaller. He was multicolored, like light, coming through a prism. The full moon is in five days. You must be out in the moonlight. Drink it in. Let it fill you. Take four stones with

you and let them soak the moonlight. This is one of them."
She pressed a tiger's-eye into my hand. "It is up to you to find
the other three."

I carried flowers with me into the short-stay surgery wing. I
saw Abby in a bed at the end of the hall. She was wide awake
and waving.

"You brought flowers," she said.

"Store-bought flowers, made to look wild," I said. "How do
you feel?"

"Good," Abby said. "Not too bad at all."

The doctor came in and leaned over the bed like an old
friend.

"Your lump was a tumor, Abby," he said.

"What kind of tumor?" she said. "What does it mean?"

"It was a malignancy," he said. "A cancer." (Sweet relief.)
"I have to tell you, of all the lumps I did today, and I did five,
yours was the one I expected least of all to be malignant."

His pager went off and he disappeared through the curtain.
It took a few seconds, but Abby turned and met my eyes.

"Cancer, huh?" she said. "My power animal was wrong."

When I had Abby tucked into her own bed I drove home
the long way, over the mountain. It was the day that would
have been John Lennon's fiftieth birthday, and on the radio
was a simulcast, the largest in history, a broadcast reaching
more people than any other broadcast had ever done. It was
live from the United Nations. Yoko Ono read a poem, and
then they played "Imagine." It was the first time I cried for
John Lennon.

Abby called me in the middle of the night.

"I know it sounds crazy," she said, "but I can't sleep without my lump. I should have asked the doctor for it. I should

have brought it home and put it under my pillow," she said. "Where do you think it has gone?"

Before her second surgery, a double mastectomy and lymph-node exploration, I took Abby down to southern Utah, to the piece of land I'd bought in the middle of nowhere because I loved it there and because having it seemed a little bit like security. My six acres is in the high desert, where it never rains except too much and more often it snows and freezes cherry blossoms or hails hard enough to make bruises on uncovered flesh. It was sage and juniper mostly, a few cacti.

Abby put her feet into the ground like she was planting them. Two ravens flew overhead in pursuit of a smaller bird, gray and blue. There was squawking, the rustle of wings, and then a clump of feathers floated down and landed at Abby's feet. Three feathers stuck together, and on each tip, a drop of blood.

Abby started singing and dancing, a song she made up as she went along, directed toward the east.

"Why do you sing and dance?" she'd once asked me. "To raise your spirits, right?" she laughed. "That is also why I sing and dance," she said. "Precisely."

She sang the same song to each of the four horizons, and danced the same steps to each with the gray bird's feathers in her hair. The words elude me now, half-English, half-Navajo. It was about light, I remember, and red dirt, and joy. When she finished dancing and turned back toward the eastern horizon the full moon rose right into her hands.

Abby looked tiny and alone in the giant white bed and among the machines she was hooked to.

"How are you?" I said.

"Not bad," she said. "A little weak. In the shamanic tradition," she said, "there is a certain amount of soul loss associated with anesthesia. Airplane travel too," she said. "Your soul can't fly fast enough to keep up. How are you?" she said. "How's Hardin?"

"He left for the Canadian Rockies this morning," I said. "He'll be gone six weeks. I asked him if he wanted to make love. He was just lying there, you know, staring at the ceiling. He said, 'I was just trying to decide whether to do that or go to Ace Hardware.' "

"I don't want you to break up with him because he would say something like that," Abby said. "I want you to break up with him because he'd say something like that and not think it was funny."

The doctor came in and started to say words like "chemotherapy," like "bone scan" and "brain scan," procedures certain to involve soul loss of one kind or another.

Simply because there was no one, I called Hardin in Canada. "That's too bad," he said, when I told him the cancer was extensive in the lymph nodes. And as usual, he was right.

The nights were getting colder, and the day after Abby got out of the hospital we picked about a thousand green tomatoes to pickle in Ball jars.

"I don't know where I want Roy to be in all of this," she said. "I know it would be too much to ask him for things like support and nurturance, so I thought about asking for things he would understand. I'd like him to stop smoking around me. I'd like him to keep our driveway free of snow."

"Those sound like good, concrete things," I said.

"I love him very much, you know," she said.

And God help me, I was jealous.

We took a walk, up towards the Uintas, where the aspen leaves had already fallen, making a carpet under our feet.

"You know," I said, "if you want to go anywhere, this year, I'll come up with the money and we'll go. It's just credit cards," I said. "I can make it happen."

"I know why my power animal lied," Abby said. "It was the intent of my question. Even though I said 'Do I have cancer?' what I meant was 'Am I going to die?' That's what I was really asking, and the answer was no."

"I'm glad you worked that out," I said.

"I've made a decision," she said. "I'm going to stop seeing the doctors."

Something that felt like a small bomb exploded in my ribs. "What do you mean?" I said.

"I'm not going to have the chemotherapy," she said. "Or any more of the tests. My power animal said I don't need them, they could even be *detrimental,* is what he said."

The sound of the dead leaves under my boots became too loud for me to bear. "Is that what he really said, Abby?" I faced her on the trail. "Did he open his mouth and say those words?"

She walked around me and went on down the trail. "You won't leave me," she said after a while. "Even if things get real bad."

I leaned over and kissed her, softly, on the head.

"I want to support her decision," I told Thomas. "I even want to believe in her magic, but she's ignoring hundreds of years of medical research. This ugly thing is consuming her and she's not doing anything to stop it."

We were walking in the moonlight on our way up to the old silver mine not far above my house. It was the harvest moon, and so bright you could see the color in the changing leaves, the red maple, the orange scrub oak, the yellow aspen. You could even tell the difference in the aspen that were yellow tinged with brown, and the ones that were yellow and still holding green.

"She is doing something," Thomas said. "She's just not doing what you want her to do."

"What, listening to her power animal?" I said. "Waiting for the spirits from the lower world to take the cancer away? How can that mean anything to me? How can I make that leap?"

"You love Abby," he said.

"Yeah," I said. The bright leaves against the dark evergreens in the moonlight were like an hallucination.

"And she loves you," he said.

"Yeah," I said.

"That's," he said, "how you make the leap."

I don't want to talk about the next few months, the way the cancer ambushed her body with more and more powerful attacks. The way she sank into her own shadow, the darkness enveloping what was left of her hair and skin. Her vitality slipping. Maybe I do want to talk about it, but not right now.

With no doctor to supply the forecasts and explanations, watching Abby's deterioration was like reading a book without a narrator, or seeing a movie in another language. Just when you thought you knew what was going on, the plot would thicken illogically.

When it all got to be too much for Roy, he moved out and I moved in. I even thought about trying to find some old ladies and teenagers, of calling some of the ladies from the Fallen Arches, thinking I could create the household Abby had wished for. It wasn't really as pathetic as it sounds. We ate a lot of good food. We saw a lot of good movies. I played my banjo and Abby sang. We laughed a lot those last days. More, I'll bet, than most people could imagine.

Abby finally even refused to eat. The world had taken everything from her she was going to let it take, and she died softly in her room one day, looking out the window at her horses.

Once I hit a rabbit in the highway, just barely hit it, I was almost able to swerve out of its way. It was nighttime, and very cold, and I stopped the car on the side of the road and walked back to where it lay dying. The humane thing, I'm told, would have been to shoot it or hit it in the head with the tire jack or run over it again. But I picked it up and held it under my coat until it died, it was only a few minutes, and it was the strangest sensation I know of, when the life all at once, it seemed, slipped away.

Abby and I didn't talk at all the day she died. She offered me no last words I could use to make an ending, to carry on with, to change my life. I held her hands for the last few hours, and then after that till they got colder than hell.

I sat with her body most of the night, without really knowing what I was looking for. An eagle, I guess, or a raven, some great huge bird bursting in a shimmer of starlight out of her chest. But if something rose out of Abby at the end, it was in a form I didn't recognize. Cartoons, she would have said, are what I wanted. Disneyland and special effects.

For two days after her death I was immobile. There was so much to be done, busy work, really, and thank goodness there were others there to do it. The neighbors, her relatives, my friends. Her stepfather and I exchanged glances several times, and then finally a hug, though I don't know if he knew who I was, or if he knew that I knew the truth about him. Her mother was the one I was really mad at, although that may have been unfair, and she and I walked circles around the house just to avoid each other, and it worked until they went back to Santa Cruz.

The third day was the full moon, and I knew I had to go outside in it, just in case Abby could see me from wherever she was. I saddled my mare for the first time in over a year and we walked up high, to the place where Abby and I had lain together under our first full moon not even a year before. My mare was quiet, even though the wind was squirrelly and we could hear the occasional footsteps of deer. She was so well behaved, in fact, that it made me wish I'd ridden her with Abby, made me hope that Abby could see us, and then I wondered why, against all indications, I still thought that Abby was somebody who had given me something to prove. *Your seat feels like a soft glove,* Abby would have said, *your horse fills it.*

I dismounted and spread some cornmeal on the ground. *Become aware, inhibit, allow.* I laid my stones so they pointed at each of the four horizons. Jade to the west, smoky quartz to the north, hematite to the south, and to the east, Abby's tiger's-eye. *Ask, receive, give.* I sang a song to the pine trees and danced at the sky. I drank the moonlight. It filled me up.

WALTZING THE CAT
Pam Houston

'Funny, sad, compassionate and true as secrets whispered between friends at night' – *Amy Bloom*

Lucy O'Rourke, is a photographer whose work takes her around the world. She is smart, funny, competent and loveable – but prone to make some very bad decisions … Her peripatetic life pitches her into raging rapids in Utah, on to the path of an alligator in the Amazon and into the eye of a Gulf Stream hurricane – not to mention a few natural disasters in the form of men. Each change of scene is a search for a home and a man with whom to establish it; each time she is disappointed anew by lovers who are afraid of commitment. Convinced that she isn't living the right life, she eventually finds a place in the Rocky Mountains, on a dilapidated ranch that just might be her safe harbour. This is the story of one woman's struggle for balance in a world that keeps pitching and rolling under her feet.

A ROUGH GUIDE TO THE HEART
Pam Houston

'Bold, energetic and exhilarating ... a stunning, stunning writer' – Mary Loudon, *The Times*

In these essays Pam Houston treats us to a celebration of real-life adventures which range over five years and five continents. But whatever Houston's destination – whether Bhutan or Bolivia or Traverse City – it is only the starting point from which she extracts her personal emotional journey. She is searching here for a place – not too safe but not too threatening – from which to negotiate mountain goats and river ice, camping trips and wine. Through her we meet some good dogs, a few good men, and the occasional grizzly.

IMPOSSIBLE SAINTS

Michèle Roberts

'*Impossible Saints*, like the life of a real saint, is dangerously close to perfection' – *Kate Saunders, Independent*

'Her fictions are high-risk, unconventional, often apparently unstable, yet are steered with such authority that the otherwise cautious reader is taken almost without realising it into dangerous and exhilarating territory … She is a writer dedicated to challenging the boundaries by which the idle and unthinking might try to circumscribe her' – *Rachel Cusk, Sunday Express*

Always bold, always provocative, Michèle Roberts turns to the forbidden pleasures and pains of the love between father and daughter and unfolds before us the life and death of Saint Josephine. Like beads in a rosary, the heady tales of other 'impossible' female saints – one-armed mad girls, beauties locked in towers, seductive daughters – are woven throughout her beguiling and passionate story.

Now you can order superb titles directly from Virago

☐	Waltzing the Cat	Pam Houston	£9.99
☐	A Rough Guide to the Heart	Pam Houston	£10.99
☐	Impossible Saints	Michèle Roberts	£6.99
☐	Fair Exchange	Michèle Roberts	£6.99
☐	The Cure for Death by Lightening	Gail Anderson-Dargatz	£6.99
☐	A Recipe for Bees	Gail Anderson-Dargatz	£6.99
☐	Little Sister	Carol Birch	£6.99
☐	Come Back, Paddy Riley	Carol Birch	£9.99
☐	Stuck up a Tree	Jenny McLeod	£6.99
☐	Like	Ali Smith	£6.99

Please allow for postage and packing: **Free UK delivery.**
Europe; add 25% of retail price; Rest of World; 45% of retail price.

To order any of the above or any other Virago titles, please call our
credit card orderline or fill in this coupon and send/fax it to:

Virago, 250 Western Avenue, London, W3 6XZ, UK.
Fax 0181 324 5678   Telephone 0181 324 5516

☐ I enclose a UK bank cheque made payable to Virago for £ ....
☐ Please charge £.............. to my Access, Visa, Delta, Switch Card No.

☐☐☐☐☐☐☐☐☐☐☐☐☐☐☐☐☐☐☐

Expiry Date ☐☐☐☐   Switch Issue No. ☐☐

NAME (Block letters please) ....

ADDRESS ....

....

....

Postcode ....Telephone ....

Signature ....

Please allow 28 days for delivery within the UK. Offer subject to price and availability.

Please do not send any further mailings from companies carefully selected by Virago ☐